Only
CHANCE
at love

MIA LONDON

ISBN 978-1-955369-02-2 ebook
ISBN 978-1-955369-03-9 pbook

Publisher: Mia London Books
PO Box 93852
Southlake, TX 76092

Edited by Traci Hall
Cover design by BookCover Kingdom

Acknowledgements

To every strong woman

Some people say I have attitude—maybe I do—but I think you have to. You have to believe in yourself when no one else does, that makes you a winner right there. ~Venus Williams

Chapter One

THE ONLINE SALES report stared back at Alexis, evidence of precisely what she'd suspected for a while. Sales for the quarter were down. Specifically, sales of shoes designed by Raffaele.

Dammit!

Alexis King was the owner and founder of AK Designs. She'd started the company ten years ago with a tiny storefront, designing shoes at her kitchen table in the off-hours while managing a l'Amour Lux fine clothing shop. Now the company had grown to four stores, two additional designers, and a huge online presence. Plus she had a new Forest Ridge location opening next month.

Running your own business was a juggle, she knew. Her investors acted like they expected the company to collapse at any minute despite the reports. She could feel the tension on every quarterly conference call. Lexi hired based on talent and experience—some of the retail staff were there for the paycheck, and the ladies liked the discount on rocking shoes.

The guys—shit! Where to start? The straight ones thought they could bang her and be in line to take over when she retired. She was thirty-nine for the love of Christ.

She sounded cynical, even to herself.

Snap out of it.

Back to Raffaele. She'd brought him on as a fresh Parsons School of Design graduate, having seen the potential within his portfolio. She'd enthused over the fact that she could train him on her way of doing business—she hated retraining those who'd been in corporate America too long, even in design.

She'd hired Raffaele and Brea about three years prior at the urging of her bestie, Rachel, who had worried that Lexi was working herself to the bone. Something had to give, and managing a business left little time for designing. Not only did AK Designs sell shoes, but handbags as well. She'd confessed to Rachel that she'd hit a creative brick wall and Rachel had suggested hiring talented young people so that Lexi could focus on the operations end.

That had been around the time of the Dillion fiasco, but she didn't want to think about that.

Raffaele's work had captivated her with his use of color and unique and interesting lines. Several shoes and bags had gone into production within months of hiring him. But lately, something was off. It was like his mind was somewhere else, or perhaps he was just bored. Lexi knew that's how it could be with creative people—lose their attention on a project and there was little hope of getting it back.

She'd spoken to him about it twice before, but any fix he'd implement was only temporary.

On the other hand, Brea didn't have an issue with the pace of designing. She was detailed and appreciated time to create without feeling rushed.

Next month, AK Designs' fifth store would open and Lexi really didn't need this stress right now. Firing a designer meant a whole host of issues cropping up, the least of which was hiring a replacement for Raffaele. What would her investors think?

It's Friday; maybe Rachel is free for a drink tonight. Chances were good Rachel would be home with Hunter and the kids. Her friend occasionally had to run an errand for her upcoming wedding, but she and Hunter weren't planning anything extravagant. In fact, she'd said they were saving all the extravagance for the honeymoon—two weeks in Australia. With all of Hunter's frequent flyer miles from work, he had enough for first-class round-trip tickets for both of them.

Australia sounded positively exquisite.

Well, no sense putting off the inevitable. Lexi picked up the phone to call Raffaele, figuring he'd be in the design/concept room—AK's playroom with sewing machines, white boards, and a plethora of leather scraps. They'd start with a conversation about a drop in sales and take it from there.

Brea answered. "Design room."

"Hey, Brea. Is Raffaele there?"

"No, sorry, Lexi. He said he had an errand to run."

That's strange. She tapped a pen on her desk. Why hadn't he told her he was leaving? "When was that?"

"Um, about an hour ago. I'm not a hundred percent sure."

Lexi sighed as she glanced at the clock: three in the afternoon. Not his normal lunch hour. "That's okay. Thanks." She disconnected the line to ring his rarely used office, as he spent most of his time in the design room. She stopped and placed the handset in the receiver, deciding to see for herself if he was in. She made the short walk down the hall not sure what she hoped to find, but maybe he'd left a note, or maybe she'd see what was distracting him from work.

She opened the door and went inside. The lights were off but other than that, the room looked as it always had—stacks of sketch pads, magazines, and various books on his desk and the floor around it. Lexi stepped farther into the space. Nothing seemed out of place. Crumpled fast-food lunch wrappers filled the waste can. No note to explain his absence.

Just as she was about to turn and leave, something caught her eye in the stack of papers on Raffaele's desk. A red and black logo.

She recognized that logo—Stiletto Inc. Stiletto was her competition and based in Kansas City. Henry Bumpass, CEO of Stiletto, had been jealous of Alexis for some time. She knew for a fact he wanted Brea on his design team, and he never got over that she'd chosen AK over Stiletto.

Lexi quickly glanced toward the door, but no one was there. Stepping closer, Lexi pushed aside the pile to reveal an envelope. She lifted it and peered inside. It appeared to be a statement; the kind that had a check attached. In this case, the check was gone. She could see by the perforated edges it had once been attached to the bottom. She tried to make sense of the words: CNSLT SRVCS.

To the far right read a dollar amount. A figure that was quite large, so it could hardly be a rebate.

Lexi scratched her head and squinted. *What is this about and why is Raffaele getting a check from Stiletto?*

She thought about the text and finally put the meaning together. It was for "consultation services."

Sonuvabitch!

Her stomach sank. Corporate espionage. No wonder he'd supposedly not been able to come up with a winning design.

She'd paid him well, gave him good benefits, treated him with respect, and this is how he repaid her? By selling secrets to the enemy?

Thoughts raced around in her head so fast she could hardly think straight.

Lexi had to get out of his office. She was in no frame of mind to confront him right then.

Her heart pounded in her chest, but she made an effort to keep her expression neutral and her legs steady. Document in hand, she passed Gregory, no doubt working hard as he always did, as she returned to her office.

She dropped into her chair with deep sadness, shoved the check stub in her drawer, and shot Raffaele a text asking him to swing by her office before leaving for the day. That was not an unusual text for her to send, so he likely wouldn't be suspicious. Of course, this would throw a monkey-wrench into whatever he was doing if he'd had no intention of returning to the office that day.

Next, she called the security team for the building and asked to have one or two officers on stand-by. She wasn't specifically fearful for Raffaele, but it was best not to take any chances.

Lexi hated this awful feeling of betrayal. She sipped in shallow breaths to ease her knotted stomach.

Whatever had she done to him? She'd chosen him as a designer and given him his own space to make a mark in the design world.

She unsuccessfully focused on combing through her email inbox, replying as needed, and scheduling an appointment for the following week.

At four a rap came at the door. Raffaele, tall and thin with disheveled hair, red Chucks, and designer denim, asked, "You wanted to see me, boss?"

Schooling her face, Lexi waved Raffaele in and dialed

security. She swiveled in her chair to hide her mouth as she spoke, "Okay, we're ready."

"Yes, ma'am," the dispatcher replied, "we'll send someone right up."

She motioned to the chair in front of her desk. "Please sit, Raffaele."

His brows furrowed, but he didn't hesitate. He crossed a foot over his knee and sat back.

"Raffaele, I don't know where to start. I'm actually rather speechless." She'd felt betrayal before, and this time was no different, but shit! She'd thought she could trust him.

His head tipped to the side, gaze innocent. Was he acting, or being a cocky SOB?

Oh, come on! "I thought you were happy. We've known each other for several years now, and well, I thought I treated you fairly. Gave you extra time when your grandma died..."

Raffaele's nose twitched like a rabbit sensing the snare.

"And made sure we had a HEPA filter for the design room to help with your allergies."

His face lost its color, knowing full-well she was onto his dirty little secret.

"I just want to know *why*. Why sell our secrets to the competition?" She didn't know who she was more upset with—Raffaele or Bumpass.

He swallowed hard. "Lexi, I'm sorry." Raffaele gulped in air like a beached fish. "I don't know why I did it."

"Not buying that. You had to know. Did you sell them

your designs too? Scratch that. I know you did and left us with the crap." Impatience and frustration bubbled up.

He glanced down and shook his head slowly. "I guess I felt important, valuable. They approached me and made it sound so easy. And they were willing to pay me..." His voice trailed off. He knew how ridiculous it sounded. He collected a great paycheck from AK.

A gentle knock rapped at the door. The armed security guard waited just outside. Lexi didn't feel like she was in danger, per se, but Raffaele had proved his actions were unpredictable at best.

She rose and smoothed her skirt. She had nothing more to say, and nothing Raffaele could say would change her mind about firing him. *Bumpass can freakin' have him.*

"So, as you can expect, this is your last day..." She strode to the door and opened it. A six-four tower of muscle stood there, his arms crossed over his tank of a chest. "This gentleman will escort you to your office to clear out your personal items."

Raffaele's shoulders slouched as he stood and made his way to his *former* office. She grabbed an empty box from the copy room to give him and watched as he loaded a few items inside. She wanted to laugh when he added several fashion magazines.

Did he really think Stiletto would hire him now? He'd proved himself a spy. She just shook her head and watched as Raffaele shuffled toward the door, his gaze downward. She held out her hand. "Key."

Everyone who had an office had a key, like Gregory and Brea. Of course, Lexi had all the duplicates and would likely have the lock changed, but it helped solidify the fact that he was gone and would never return.

He handed her the office key, and with sadness in his eyes, said, "I'm sorry."

She had no response. He'd disappointed her beyond belief.

Chapter Two

LEXI SHOULD STILL be burning mad, but instead, the icy chill of managing the backstabbing had thawed to a slow burn.

"I'm so over this," Alexis said to no one as she slammed the top drawer of her desk closed and locked it.

What a freakin' lousy day! What a way to end the week!

Brea would need to know what happened, but that could wait until Monday.

It was Friday, and she'd hoped to have a weekend to herself before the launch. Now, she'd likely be combing the job sites for another designer. Ever since she'd started her company, Alexis rarely had a free weekend but had no regrets. She loved AK Designs more than she loved just about anything, though it was starting to wear on her.

She needed a vacation. She'd never been to Switzerland. Hell, if she could carve out several weeks, she'd travel Europe to fill the creative well. Until then, she could use a distraction of epic proportions.

Lexi might not be able to vacation just yet, especially being short a designer, but at least she had time for a drink. She thought about calling Rachel or Milo, but really, she was emotionally exhausted. She just needed to unwind with a whiskey before driving home and starting again tomorrow.

She walked to the parking garage, got into her Lexus, then headed to her favorite bar, Bogart's, a few short miles from her office. It was an upscale place Alexis could pop into when she needed to decompress. She didn't go out often because—no offense to men—she was sick of getting hit on.

Maybe I should buy a CZ ring, and everyone will think I'm married?

Most men, Lexi figured, fit into three categories. The first group were intimidated by her—her designer clothes, nice figure, attractive face. And she knew she didn't make it easy for them. They heard CEO and founder of a successful, growing company and fumbled over their words. Their weakness reminded her of her exes. The second category had the gold-diggers—those men who recognized her wealth and saw dollar signs instead of the interesting, engaging woman behind the position. The third group held losers who thought more highly of themselves than they should. They'd worked their way to middle-management, perhaps, listened to self-help books during their commute, and couldn't hold a conversation with a woman without making it about themselves. Waste of her time!

She hung her new find—a vintage Prada—on the back of

the barstool and sidled into her favorite spot at the end of the bar, away from the chaos. Most everyone gathered at the far end, on their feet, eyes glued to the TV. "Marker's Mark and 7UP, Josh," Lexi called to the bartender.

He lifted his chin in acknowledgement.

"How you doin', sweetheart?" Josh placed a drink on a cocktail napkin and slid it in front of her.

She took a sip. Josh made a good pour. Of course, it helped that she tipped him well. Josh and the laidback yet still-upscale atmosphere, were the reasons she could relax in this place.

Josh had let her know that he was available for a quick lay, if Lexi wanted. He was a good-looking guy, fun to flirt with, and about her age. But she didn't want to fuck up a great business relationship. Literally.

"Hell of a week. Had to fire a designer today." Unwind tonight, because tomorrow she'd need to get the creative juices going and pull out her sketch pad.

Josh grimaced. "Bummer. Stay here as long as you can stand it. I have to warn you, though. The game's on, and this crowd is live tonight."

A shout sounded from a high-top table, followed by a whistle. Yeah, it might be a short night. "Thanks." Lexi wasn't much of a basketball fan.

She sighed as a guy in an ill-fitted suit, a receding hairline, and stupid-ass swagger approached her. She'd walked through the front door—what?—three or four minutes prior. *This might be a new record.*

"Hey, sugar." The man adjusted his ten-year-old tie. "Haven't I seen you someplace before?"

"Yes. That's why I don't go there anymore." Definitely Category Three.

"Ooh, touchy. Okay, I can take a hint. But if you're still lonely at the end of the night and need some lovin', I'll be right over there." The guy pointed into the shadows of the bar. She had no idea exactly where and didn't care. She set her face and waited for him to leave.

After he retreated, she took a healthy gulp of her drink savoring the aroma and subtle burn as the whiskey made its way down. She may have moaned at the exquisiteness. It could have been the drink or the fact that she was long overdue for some alone time with her favorite bourbon. *Yum.*

Another man approached who scanned her body head to toe as if that was a turn-on. She'd peg him as in the first category. His hesitancy before speaking to her directly told her all she needed to know.

He leaned his elbow on the bar top. "Hey, bud. Can I get a martini?"

Oh, he wants to look like a power-player, she thought.

Alexis lifted her phone to her ear, making her voice loud enough to be heard by her unwanted admirer. "Why the hell are you calling?" She paused for effect. "Look. You can either sell me your company at the price I offered, or everyone will know what a sham you are by close of business Monday. And for good measure, I'll publish the pictures I took of your minuscule penis. It'll be viral within forty-eight hours." She glanced briefly at the guy to her left and narrowed her eyes. "Fuckin' right. I want that contract signed before your wife comes home." She pretended to end the call and sighed. "Asshole prick," she said into her glass before she took another swig, catching a glimpse of the guy next to her. His face was ashen. He gripped the drink Josh left him and returned to his table without saying a word.

Josh grinned at her. "They're on to you tonight, babe. I'm nominating you for an Oscar."

Lexi couldn't stop herself from snickering. It really was just a game to her. She'd resigned herself to living alone for the rest of her life. She'd likely never find her match. She'd retire on beachfront property someday, get off on the cabana boys waiting on her every desire, and have a cat. Or maybe a dog. Did it matter? Dog, they're more cuddly.

When the ballgame returned after the halftime break, another bartender raised the volume, and all eyes turned toward the big screen TV. Alexis combed the bar, searching for anything interesting to distract her. Looked to be about eighty percent men, twenty percent women.

Hot damn! One woman had on a pair of *her* shoes. She loved it when that happened. Lexi smiled.

"You have a great smile."

Her head snapped to the voice at her right, the only other seat at the end of the bar. Where the fuck had he come from?

The stranger sat in the seat beside her and nodded toward Josh.

"Hey, Derek, how's it going?" Josh gave him a fist bump.

"Good, man. Can I get a Sierra Nevada pale ale? No glass." Derek was tall, maybe six-three, with good muscle tone, like a gym rat.

"You bet." Josh pivoted away to get the beer.

As Derek reached into his jeans pocket and set his phone on the bar, he glanced at her and said, "You're welcome."

She raised an eyebrow. "Excuse me?"

He looked up from his phone. "I paid you a compliment, you said 'thank you,' and I replied, 'you're welcome.'" His confident smile showed straight, white teeth that left Alexis momentarily speechless.

Arrogant much? "I did?"

The crowd yelled and screamed at the TV. Something good must have happened.

"I'm boiling it down." He shrugged his shoulder. "If I recall correctly, it was more like 'thank you for noticing. I'm immersed in a boring life, and it's nice to have someone care enough to pull me from the monotony.'"

Well, crap. She might be mildly attracted to this guy. She forced herself to focus on his game. She ruled out Category One. Maybe Category Two or Three? But on some level, he intrigued her. Maybe she needed a new category...

His words also struck a chord within her.

He flashed his smile, and she let the corners of her lips curve slightly in response.

"Monotony, huh?"

"Sure." Derek eyed Josh. "Thanks, man." He saluted her and took a gulp from his bottle. "From the looks of you—"

Ah-hah! Category Two: gold digger.

"You're very successful. You're dressed like you just came from work. Perhaps after having a bad day? You're probably in no rush to get home. You work your ass off and aren't appreciated. You sometimes question why you work so hard, even if you love your job. And life has become tedious and mind-numbing."

Shit! He might have hit the nail on the head.

She sipped her drink. "Perhaps. And of course, you already know you sound cocky in your assessment."

Ignoring her statement, Derek leaned close, so close she could feel his hot breath on her neck. "And you come here for entertainment and escapism, and maybe, just maybe, a challenge."

A shiver raced down her spine.

Now that was an interesting take on things.

How long had he been watching her? Her heart kicked over. Was he a stalker?

Wait! Was that a Tag watch on his wrist? *Not* Category Two.

What's this guy's scheme?

"A challenge?" She lifted her eyebrows.

"You like a challenge don't you, sweetheart?"

Is he trying to be condescending? She narrowed her eyes.

"I mean no disrespect. I am incredibly attracted to strong women." His eyes, hazel, were sincere. "I would never say anything to hurt you." Derek eased back a few inches. "The question remains—do you like a challenge?"

Lexi licked her lips. That was a loaded question. And she didn't know how to answer it. Half of her wanted to tell him to fuck off. The other half wanted to accept whatever challenge he thought would make her think life wasn't tedious and mind-numbing.

The crowd got raucous again. Nevertheless, she lowered her voice and leveled him a look. "I love a challenge."

Derek sat back in his barstool and took a long draw off his beer, his full lips pressed against the bottle as he studied her.

Nice watch, manicured hands, but worn jeans, basic T-shirt, and mischievous smile. This guy was an enigma.

Her nether parts awakened when she thought about those lips against her instead of that bottle.

She glanced back at the crowd—a sea of backs. Everyone's attention was glued to the TV. A few women chatted in a far corner, not caring about their surroundings. Three guys in game shirts leaned on the bar and impatiently waited for their drink refills.

Derek slid his barstool closer, his legs straddling her chair to get closer. "So, here's the challenge, beautiful, should you choose to accept it…"

He faced her side with his arm on the back of her barstool. His spicy scent imbued her senses and clouded her brain. *Focus!*

"Right here in this bar, I will make you come without touching your skin."

Lexi gasped. Her head spun to meet his gaze dead in the eyes, their faces mere inches apart. She blinked.

"What the fuck?" Was this guy serious?

Derek gave her a slight yet confident smile. He *was* serious. He ran the back of his finger over her thigh and up again. Heat from his light caress penetrated the fine wool fabric of her skirt.

"Over clothing, not touching your skin. You don't move from that chair. Do you accept?"

She clamped her mouth closed and inhaled through her nose to calm her racing heart.

Lexi scanned the patrons in the bar to see if this was a joke. She couldn't actually entertain this outrageous offer from a handsome stranger in torn jeans and an expensive watch. Nobody was watching them—they were literally alone in the crowd.

She swiped her bottom lip. It had been too long since she'd been with a man. Ugh, her sex life was mediocre at best. His words, his actions, already had her hotter than her last encounter, and she hadn't been wearing any clothes then! "And if you can't?"

He pursed his full mouth as if that was an impossible outcome. Talk about arrogant. "If I can't make you come, I'll buy you dinner at a restaurant of your choosing."

"Nice try. You want a date." She scrunched up her face at him but was still intrigued.

Leaning close to her ear, he whispered, "I could have said 'if I don't make you come through your clothes, I get to try without your panties in the way'." He didn't pull back—just waited for her to answer his proposal.

Oh, shit. His words melted over her like warm ganache.

She cradled her tumbler. *What to do.* Alexis had never had an offer like this before. So blatant. So risky. So erotic.

If it went south, she'd have to find a freakin' new bar—she glanced up at Josh, mixing drinks for patrons—*and* a new bartender.

He was a stranger—a cocky, witty, sexy stranger, but still... Josh seemed to know Derek, that had to count for something.

Her heart hammered in her chest. *What the hell.* She nodded.

"You have to say it. I accept your challenge to make me come in this bar, Derek."

Lexi let out a shaky breath. "I accept your challenge to make me come, through my clothes." She might be a risk-taker, but hell, this had to be the raciest thing she'd ever done.

He ran a finger up and down her arm through her silk blouse. He murmured, his mouth inches from her ear, "Take a sip of your drink."

She did as he commanded, anxious to see what he'd do next.

"Don't worry," Derek said, still stroking up and down her arm. "No one can see. They're watching the game."

He rose and moved behind her, his arms encompassing her. His hands slid along the outside of her skirt, smoothing her thighs and her hips. After several passes, he inched the skirt upward. Her nipples peaked.

"What's your name, beautiful?"

"Alexis."

"Alexis, keep your gorgeous eyes forward."

Forward. Right. She wouldn't look down to see how much thigh he was revealing. She could feel the coolness of skin bared, and she feared her black satin panties might soon be visible.

Well, not very *visible* in a dark bar under the shadows of the bar top.

Still, she felt incredibly exposed. And incredibly wet.

"Spread your legs and lean forward, elbows on the bar," he whispered in her ear.

She shifted on the bar stool, feeling a bit more concealed in this position. She scanned the bar. No one paid them any attention. Josh and the other bartender worked frantically to fill orders for the thirsty, rowdy crowd.

Derek's hands skimmed her torso, over her blouse, making his way upward. "What I wouldn't do to touch your amazing skin with my bare hands. Feel how soft it is." His thumbs glazed over her hard nipples poking against her bra. "To hold your breasts in my hands, massaging them, tasting them, learning how responsive they would be under my tongue."

She moaned at the erotic images his words conveyed and arched slightly into his hands. She kept her gaze forward, along the long bar top, occasionally glancing at the TV and Josh. To anyone looking their way, they appeared as a couple canoodling and whispering sweet nothings.

Ha! Nothing sweet going on here.

Derek Hollister placed a kiss on top of Lexi's shoulder over her silk blouse and returned to his seat. His hands missed the warmth from cupping her breasts.

When he'd first spied Alexis at Bogart's two months ago, he'd wanted to meet her, but it hadn't been the right time.

In his brief observation, Alexis—Lexi, as her friend had called her—had an elegant and confident disposition Derek found incredibly attractive. She'd appeared somewhat selective of who she'd talked with at the engagement party. She laughed, but not too loud. Had drinks but didn't get drunk. He studied her stylish attire and manicured appearance. It was clear she had money.

God, he could read her like a book. He wasn't after

money; it only appealed to him because it meant she was a go-getter.

He'd visited the bar a few times, some days congratulating himself for the patience and resilience on expecting to see her again. Other days, chiding himself because he only assumed she lived in town but maybe she didn't. He couldn't explain why he was so drawn to her, he just knew he had to meet her.

He draped his left arm on the back of her chair, and his right hand rested on her hip over her bunched skirt. "Take another sip." He wanted her relaxed and not worried about any potential audience.

She lifted the glass and brought it to her mouth.

He grabbed his beer, swallowing deep. The drink felt cool gliding into his fiery insides. Then, he slid his hand over her hip joint, down her center, to the apex of her thighs.

She sucked air in through her nostrils.

"You feel like a woman ready to explode. Hot and wet. You probably taste better than the finest bourbon." Derek smoothed a single digit over her slit and up to her tiny bundle of nerves. He wanted her craving more.

Alexis parted her legs and pressed into his hand.

He could hear her gentle panting over the crowd and TV. He would do this. He would make her come. A fantasy come true.

"Good girl. You feel amazing." He applied a scant more pressure. He ran a smooth line up and down, grazing over her clit and across her lips.

"Oh fuck," she breathed.

"Ride my fingers if you want. You're beautiful, and I bet sexy as hell when you come."

She moaned as he added more pressure, smoothing over her in tiny circles. She twitched; the beginnings of her climax worked to the surface.

The triumph washed over him. "Beautiful, I will be here next week. Same day, same time. Wear a skirt and no panties. I forgot to tell you, that's what I get if I win the challenge."

Her eyes widened.

There was no turning back. She covered the moan with her hands, gasping for air as her climax ricocheted through her.

When she settled, he pushed her skirt into place and relaxed on his stool.

She glanced his way. A beautiful glow flushed her cheeks.

He shook his head. "Incredible."

Her eyes shifted to the bulge in the front of his jeans. Derek wouldn't hide it. She was sexy and gorgeous, and he wanted more.

"Thank you."

"No. *Thank you*." He flashed a smile.

Alexis bit on her plump lower lip. She knew, he'd won. He secured another chance to see, a chance to get to know this woman he'd only dreamed about until now.

He winked at her, then yanked the wallet from his pocket, placed a hundred-dollar bill on the bar top for Josh as he rose, grabbing his phone and keys. "Next week, same day, no panties." He leaned down to kiss her cheek. "And wear a poncho."

She wrinkled her brow.

Oh yeah, baby. I have plans. But before she could ask, he left.

Chapter Three

DEREK PATIENTLY WAITED for the elevator to his office on the sixth floor Monday morning. Vigers Tech, an infrastructure and internet hardware company, occupied the entire fourth, fifth, and sixth floors of the PetroChem building in downtown Houston. Derek was the company's CFO and go-to-answer-man.

Some days he couldn't wait to get to work. Like when the international financial markets were a flurry of activity, the company launched a new product, or The Fed announced a rate reduction.

All accounting and treasury functions reported to him, in addition to asset management, which included Vigers' manufacturing sites and their two call centers. Basically, the financial health of the company rested on his shoulders.

This week, it was business as usual with nothing exciting in the works. The polar opposite of his weekend, which had been the best he'd had in a long time. A *very* long time.

His patience waiting to finally meet Alexis in person had

paid off.

Friday night she'd walked into Bogart's. Alone. He somehow knew, if she were alone, she'd stay away from the throng of people.

She'd perched at the far end of the bar, away from the TV-watching crowd. Men had hit on her, and she shot them down. One by one.

He'd known he'd need a winning game plan to grab and keep Lexi's attention. He'd learned from his mentor, Renee, years ago, the subtleties of seducing a woman. Some women required a delicate touch. And some, like Lexi, needed someone to take the reins for a while. But only in a way that meant more to them by giving up that power and control. It had to be worth it.

If he intended to strike up a conversation, well, it would have to be good. He had one fucking shot at this.

That night when he'd conjured up the idea of the offer, he knew it would have to be something audacious and over-the-top. It had to shake her up and set her on edge. *Not* the kind of edge she seemed to get from men who approached her. Those poor guys wouldn't know what to do with a woman like Lexi.

Derek was very good at reading people. He took a chance and called her bored with her routine and frustrated, possibly fulfilled with her job, but not in her personal life. Hence the challenge. He liked a challenge too and saw himself in her that way. But what he'd offered—whoa!—had been risky as hell.

And it had paid off! His plan to seduce her had worked and now he had a "date" with her in five days.

He'd taken his fair share of women to bed. He'd loved every minute of it, but none of them had the spunk that Lexi had. Some men may be intimidated by her. Not Derek. The challenge she presented only fueled him.

He had his sights set on Alexis, and he would have her.

Derek strode into his oversized office—really, it was a waste of space—and brought his PC to life. His assistant, Marta, had helped decorate the room years ago—company awards on the bookshelves, framed art above his leather sofa, and a large potted plant by the window.

He slid into his leather chair, contemplating his day, and opened his calendar.

Derek had poured his energies into being the best in his career, and now he wanted something more...something personal. He had the castle and the cars, but no one to share them with. That might have been something he recognized in Lexi too—she was driven but seemed on the verge of burnout.

They could be good together; he'd just need to convince her to give them a chance. He didn't dare think about his upcoming date with Lexi—getting hard at work was incredibly indiscreet.

Marta poked her head through the doorway.

"Good morning."

"Morning, Derek. Just letting you know I'm here. You

have an open schedule until ten-thirty. There are a few things for your approval on email," she gestured with her chin to his computer, "but otherwise buzz me if you need me."

"Will do. Thanks."

Lexi sat at her desk Monday morning, reprimanding herself. Her entire weekend had been useless as she couldn't get Derek out of her head.

What the hell was I thinking? A stranger! She'd replayed her Friday night at Bogart's with Derek over and over.

Extraordinary bliss had raced through her, warming her entire body, letting go of months of pent-up desire, pent-up frustration. She'd been equally impressed with his skill and embarrassed that she let it happen.

She'd had a full agenda for the weekend—finding a replacement for Raffaele, drafting some new shoe and bag designs, errands, plus dinner Sunday at Rachel's. But the images, the tenor of Derek's voice, his scent, and the incredible sensations he'd provided had flooded her entire being.

She'd been tempted to tell Rachel about it, but with Rachel's fiancé and the kids there, she'd decided to wait. Not to mention, this could be a one-and-done scenario. Why a man like Derek had chased her, she didn't know. Why wasn't he married? Tall, handsome, and successful, why was he still single? In his forties, she guessed. Probably divorced then.

Unless he was Category Four, which Lexi *hated* to think about. All the cheaters. Dillion and Bryan were Category Four, and she hadn't seen it coming. She had been so blinded by love—ugh!—she almost gagged on the thought of what a fool she'd been. Never again.

Or could she say that? Didn't Raffaele now fit into that category?

Derek hadn't worn a ring, so she had to believe he was unattached. She'd ask.

Lexi sighed. They were to meet again on Friday. A little thrill raced through her. She could cross one thing off her list for the week—she'd purchased a poncho. How completely satiating it was to be with a man who knew how to please her.

Maybe it had been too long since her last romp, but Derek was offering so she'd take him up on it. As long as it was strictly physical, everything would be absolutely perfect.

Lexi's office phone rang, pulling her from her daydreams. Gregory, her comptroller. He ran all her accounts, and Lexi trusted him because he'd time and again shown his loyalty to her with late hours if needed and triple-checking reports. Not to mention, he'd never once tried to hit on her.

"Hey, Lexi. Just wanted to give you a heads-up—we're almost done with the audit. Then if you want, we can sit down and go over next year's budget."

"Great. I'm looking forward to it. Oh, Gregory?" She swiveled on her chair.

"Yeah?"

"I fired Raffaele Friday afternoon. He'd been selling secrets and designs to Stiletto."

"What the fuck?" Gregory exhaled. "Sorry."

"No, it's okay." Lexi almost chuckled. Gregory wasn't much of a curser which showed his level of surprise. "I said the same thing. So, anyway, I'm on the hunt for his replacement."

"Okay, got it, boss."

She disconnected the line and pressed the call button for Tonia, her assistant. The stylish brunette was in her early thirties, witty, and she'd proved over the last five years to be one of the best hires Alexis had ever made. Tonia had married a man who treated her like a princess, and they had three young kids. Lexi had no idea how she managed them all.

"Hello, Lexi."

"Tonia, I need a quick trip to Kansas City. Would you please book me a flight for a morning departure tomorrow or Wednesday? Whatever works better in my calendar. The return can be two or three hours later."

"You got it."

"Thanks." She and Bumpass would have a little tete-a-tete. He was probably still jealous or upset about her hiring Brea. Well, enough of that crap.

She rang the design room for Brea.

"Hi, Lexi."

"Hey, Brea. Can you break away for lunch today?"

"Um, yeah."

She heard the hesitancy in Brea's voice. They didn't often go out for lunch. In fact, quite often Lexi had lunch brought in for anyone working in the design room.

"Great. I'll see you then."

At nearly noon, Brea knocked on her doorjamb. Lexi looked up to see Brea in a colorful top, black ankle-length pants, and last year's chunky heels. "Hey. Ready?"

Walking out of the building, they headed east for a few blocks toward a great casual Pho place with fast service.

Lexi started the conversation. "I'm sure you're wondering what this is about."

Brea glanced over with a closed-mouth smile on her lips. "It's Raffaele."

Brea slung her large, eggplant AK handbag over her shoulder. One of her first designs at AK and still a top seller.

"I fired him Friday."

"Oh, wow."

"He was selling secrets and designs to Stiletto."

Brea's jaw dropped.

Lexi adjusted her sunglasses. "I'm not quite sure what was going on, what made him decide to do that, but I wanted to tell you in person."

Brea nodded.

"I also wanted to make sure you're happy at the company."

Brea nibbled on the inside of her cheek. "Are you going

to hire a replacement?"

"Yes, eventually. I want to find the right fit."

"Okay. To answer your question, I'm very happy."

They arrived at the restaurant and were seated immediately. After water was served, Brea said, "I don't know what was up with Raffaele because we weren't close. I'm sorry he did that." She sipped from her glass. "But AK is my home and I have ideas..."

"Ideas?" The young woman always had ideas which was something Lexi admired. Brea had more creativity in her pinky finger than Lexi had in her whole body.

Brea pulled a mini- sketch pad from her bag. "I haven't had time to flush out the whole thing yet, but I'm thinking of calling it 'The Brea Collection'."

Lexi smiled; she liked the sound of that. Brea's designs sold and she was glad to give credit where it was due.

Brea flipped open her book. Sketched on the pages were shoes, some flats, some heels, plus accessories like bags and belts.

"Wow," Lexi breathed out.

Brea's cheeks turned pink. "I could do a new collection every year, maybe even coordinate it with the Pantone Color of the Year, plus black of course, and you know..." she trailed off.

Talented Brea had a shy side. She was thoughtful in her creation, took her time, and loved seeing an idea come to fruition.

Lexi flipped the pages. "These are great. I love the idea." It was true.

Brea sat taller. "You do?"

"Definitely. When can we be ready for a prototype?"

Brea giggled, showing her youth and enthusiasm.

It was clear Brea had no interest in going anywhere else. Lexi beamed inside. Knowing the issue with Raffaele was an isolated event gave her incredible peace of mind.

Brea chatted on about her ideas and the possibility of getting a 3D printer for the design room. As they ate, the conversation shifted to light-hearted personal stuff.

Lexi glowed inside after their lunch. *I should do this more often with my employees.*

~

Lexi's flight landed in Kansas City. With her purse in hand, she walked outside to grab a ride to see her nemesis.

This whole issue of hiring Raffaele to supply AK Design secrets needed to be dealt with quickly and succinctly. She would confront the CEO of Stiletto Inc., Henry Bumpass, in person. She'd make it abundantly clear she didn't play games, and if he pulled anything like this again, she'd hang him by his balls in the middle of town.

Her first reaction had been to hire a PI to dig up some dirt on the man—if he stooped low, she could stoop lower. But ultimately, she didn't really want to take up the mindshare nor did she have the inclination to bother with the dickhead. No, she'd just confront his ass and tell him to stay the hell out of her company.

The driver pulled up in front of the unimpressive two-story gray building with a cracked concrete parking lot and overgrown landscaping. Proof that perhaps this company was struggling.

Lexi handed some cash to the driver, a twenty-something young woman with a ponytail, a ring tattoo, and perfect tails on her black eyeliner. "Do me a favor? Wait for me, please. This won't take long at all."

"Sure," the driver said. "I'll wait."

Lexi strode through the front door to the receptionist in the lobby. She noted the simple tiled flooring, outdated drapes, and a large black and red Stiletto logo hanging behind the desk. The space certainly didn't convey fashion-forward enterprise. "Can you direct me to Mr. Bumpass's office?"

"Take the elevator up to the second floor." The receptionist pointed to the hall on her right. "His assistant will help you from there."

Oh, yes, she will.

Arriving on the second floor, Lexi made the short walk down the hallway and found an open, carpeted area. The assistant's desk was a high-gloss walnut, the waiting-area chairs had taut cushions and current fabric, and lush plants were grouped in the corner by the wall of newly washed windows. A stark contrast from the lobby area.

So, this is where the money he made off my company is

going to. Upgrading the furnishings is probably just a tip of the iceberg.

His assistant, dressed in a tailored fuchsia suit and perfect makeup, looked up at her. "Hello. May I help you?"

Lexi had been spotlighted a few times in smaller business or regional magazines and interviewed on several morning talk shows. She breathed a sigh of relief that Henry's assistant didn't recognize her as the owner and CEO of their competition.

The next step, getting through Henry's door when she didn't have an appointment. She leaned forward as if telling the young woman a secret. "Yes, well, it's a rather a private matter." She glanced to the right, then left. "I was hoping to have a moment with Mr. Bumpass to discuss his wife's gambling debts."

The woman's face lost all color and her head rocked back on her neck. "Oh my." She quickly peered at his closed office door. "He's free right now. Why don't you just go on in?"

"Oh, thanks. I really appreciate your help with this matter." She faked a smile of sincerity. The lie was nothing. Sometimes it was a necessary evil to get past the gatekeeper. Lexi had vindication on her mind.

Lexi opened the door where Henry Bumpass, scumbag, sat behind a cluttered desk as he watched something on the internet. His belly forced him back from the desk, and his ill-fitting suit and loud tie made him look like a used car salesman. He raised his gaze and noticeably swallowed.

She pushed the door closed, strode over the worn carpeting to press her fists against the edge of his desk.

Bumpass silenced the computer speakers and leaned back in his chair. "What are *you* doing here? I should call security," he said in a gruff voice.

The problem with that was Lexi wouldn't be intimidated. He'd hired one of *her* employees and paid him to give away her company secrets.

"Good, you recognize me," which she already knew he would. Industry events make it impossible to avoid your competition. "So I'll cut right to it. I know what you did and I'm here to tell you to stay away from my company. In fact, stay out of my town. You are a low-life who—"

"Now watch it there, missy." He rose and pointed a finger in her face.

She ignored his idle threat and continued, "You are a low-life who can't create a successful company on your own, so you steal secrets from your competition. It's pathetic."

He scoffed. "You can't prove a thing."

She smiled like the Grinch on Christmas Eve after he'd hatched his plan. "You'd like to think I can't."

She stood tall and crossed her arms over her chest, feeling her blood pressure climb. "Was he worth it? Did you get your money's worth?" referring to Raffaele. "Perhaps you're still sore about losing Brea to me."

Bumpass' face turned red, but his lips clamped shut.

She shook her head and nearly *tsked*. "In addition to my lawyers, Condé Nast is on stand-by. They're always up for a juicy story. Consider this your shot over the bow. Stay away from my company, or I will make you bleed." She strung out the last four words.

His mouth gaped.

She knew she'd made her point and nothing more was necessary. If Bumpass was smart, he'd heed her warning and keep clear of Houston.

She opened his office door, strode down the hall—in a far-superior shoe than Stiletto would ever make—and pressed the button for the elevator. The assistant sputtered but Lexi didn't look back.

That had to be the shortest meeting ever on record. And probably the most satisfying. She got back into her waiting ride, gratification flowing over her. Her driver pivoted toward her in surprise to see Lexi so soon.

"To the airport, please."

"Yes, ma'am." She cleared her throat. "You seem in great spirits. Must have been a good meeting."

She called it perfectly.

"Indeed, it was," Lexi replied with a smile.

Chapter Four

FRIDAY NIGHT, DEREK was already seated at the bar in Bogart's. Waiting for me, Lexi thought with a thrill of satisfaction. Had he worried she would back out on his second challenge?

Good. She slid onto the vacant stool next to him. "Lucky for you my plans got canceled for this evening."

"Hello." Derek rose slightly as she got comfortable, scanning her body, likely assessing her attire.

She wore a straight skirt, shorter than last time, decadent high heels, and a button-down silk blouse, laying the freakin' poncho she bought over her lap.

The heat of his stare made her lower belly clench. God, she was crazy for doing this. But she wanted it, which was even crazier...

"Canceled?"

She lifted a brow, daring him to call her bluff. But, of course, she was bluffing. She'd had no plans for the evening. She would have likely done some work—sketching and combing portfolios for potential new hires—and fallen asleep in front of the television. But she wasn't used to taking orders from anyone, let alone a man. Holding onto some semblance of control gave Lexi peace of mind. If this delicious entanglement could stay physical, with no false promises of more, she'd consider playing along for a while. She'd sworn to never let a man take possession of her emotions again.

A new bartender approached. "What can I get 'cha?" She wondered if Josh had the night off.

"A glass of your driest chardonnay." She saved the hard stuff for the really bad days.

The bartender nodded and left.

"Well, I consider myself lucky that you made it then." The corner of Derek's scrumptious mouth lifted.

Shit! Her insides were on fire. Where was that wine?

She merely smiled, schooling her expression. When her wine arrived, Derek lifted his whiskey glass. He didn't say a word. His gaze penetrated her, but he uttered no tacky toast, offered no ridiculous phrase to mark the moment—just a simple tap of tumbler to glass as he let his eyes do all the talking.

And, boy, did he have something to say.

Lexi's mind raced with questions, with lust, with anticipation.

She sipped her wine, getting her bearings as she observed the once-again crowded bar. Most everyone huddled at the far end, attention glued to the big screen television.

"So," he said, "how was your week at work?"

"Better." It had been too, as they all learned to adjust without Raffaele.

"Good. Same for me, although being here was all I could think about."

She held his gaze and swallowed. Admittedly, meeting Derek had been in her thoughts as well. His eyes were a mesmerizing, brilliant hazel with just enough umber to keep them from being green. She'd never seen anything like it. The deep, penetrating eyes, the confident smile, the strength in his jaw—his looks stole her breath away.

He shifted his barstool closer to her, his hand resting on the back of her chair. "Alexis, those are some of the sexiest shoes I've ever seen on a woman." He leaned in to whisper, "I would love nothing more than to fuck you wearing only those sexy heels." Then he slowly trailed his tongue over the shell of her ear, sending a shiver straight down her spine.

Her body quivered under his touch. Alexis had no idea how much he wanted to make her quiver.

Derek's heart pounded a little faster than usual, sitting next to this gorgeous woman. Her brown hair with highlights, blue eyes, and kissable, full lips made her the envy of any woman within a fifty-mile radius. Derek kept it casual tonight with loose slacks and a polo shirt, untucked.

After waiting over thirty minutes, he wasn't sure she'd

show. He had to fucking believe Alexis wanted more, that the taste the prior week couldn't have been enough. He had an inkling she was a risk-taker and perhaps a little bored in her life. He wanted to worship her, to show her how taking a risk could pay off so incredibly.

A couple took the seats several feet away along the front of the bar.

He felt Alexis tense, and she licked her lips. He grazed a thumb over her shoulder. Would she change her mind?

She met his gaze.

"It doesn't matter about them." The couple was there to watch the game. Would Alexis trust him? "Did you leave your panties at home?"

"I guess you'll find out." Her sassy tongue enflamed him, challenged him.

And fuck, how he loved a challenge.

"Same deal as last time. If you can't make me come, dinner's on you," she stated, meeting his gaze dead-on. She wasn't about to be intimidated by the possibility of an audience.

A tiny ping set off deep inside. Her fiery nature, her wit, told him she was the perfect woman for playing in his field. "Looking forward to it."

"First, a question."

"Okay." He lifted an eyebrow.

"Are you married?"

It was a sound question, and he should have expected it.

"No. You?"

"No."

"Great. Then we're two consenting, unattached adults enjoying each other's company."

She nodded, seemingly satisfied.

His hand slid over her thigh beneath her black, fine-knit poncho resting on her lap. He stroked her warm flesh over her skirt for several moments.

She sipped her wine and faced the crowded bar, making sure no eyes were on them.

"Put your poncho on."

She sucked in her lower lip and did as he asked. It was summer in Houston and warm outside. Normally, people might think twice about her wearing a black knit drape, but bars were often chilly with air conditioning so he doubted anyone would even notice.

He rose and took a casual position behind her, her spicy perfume filling his nostrils. His hands stroked her thighs and up the sides of her torso under the drape, letting them roam over her belly to just under her breasts. She wore a bra; he'd secretly hoped she wouldn't.

"Push forward in your seat, Alexis. I want to see if you followed the rules."

As she moved toward the edge of the stool, she whispered back, "I follow my own rules."

Feisty. How he loved independent, smart women who didn't take shit from anyone.

He shimmied her skirt higher up her thighs, and for the first time, his fingertips met her soft, warm skin. His dick strained behind his zipper.

Each hand caressed her skin, slowly working her skirt up her legs to bunch on her thighs. Then, he parted them.

An oath escaped on her breath.

He'd leave her in this position for just a bit, allowing the subtle scent of hot woman fill his senses.

His hands crept back under the black cover and worked loose the buttons on her blouse.

She didn't stop him, perhaps understanding no one could see what he was doing. But as he moved higher, it would be obvious. "Elbows on the bar, gorgeous."

Her elbows rested on the bar top, and she clasped her hands in front of her mouth, staring in the direction of the TV.

Now, with the fabric falling in front of her torso, he had free reign to claim those sumptuous breasts trapped in their casing.

With every button unfastened, he pulled her blouse apart. His hands cupped her breasts, toying gently with the hard nubs eager for his touch. He only teased her another moment when he drew the satin down, allowing her breasts to pop free.

He played with her tight nipples, staring straight ahead as if they were both enjoying the game. That was the furthest thing from his mind. Her chest arching into his hands and her soft mewls were what he'd come to hear.

"Head to the side," he whispered in her right ear.

She tipped her head left, giving him access to the delicate skin of her neck. He kissed, licked, and sucked her, all while caressing her breasts and nipples and completely neglecting her over-anxious pussy.

Finally, he dragged his hands to her naked, spread thighs, stroking the inside and out of her soft, creamy skin. "Fuck, you feel so good."

"Mmm," was her only reply.

With each pass on her thighs, he pushed her skirt higher. He knew what he was doing, how he was pushing her far beyond her comfort zone.

Just another inch, and her skirt was fully gathered up and over her pussy.

She whimpered but didn't stop him. Instead, she tensed under his touch.

"Relax, baby. I'm about to give you the most incredible climax you've ever had," he murmured in her ear.

To up the intrigue, he pulled her legs as far as they would go and let his hands roam.

Oh fuck, she was so smooth. So utterly completely smooth and naked for him. He loved that she'd done what he'd asked, knowing she'd come here for him, to receive what he had to give her.

He stroked her delectable skin, not giving her what he was sure she was desperate for.

Teasing her was also killing him. He had to know how wet she was, had to feel all of her. He wanted to see her fully naked, but that would have to wait. He had a plan, a way to rope her in and draw her closer. This bar was merely a steppingstone.

His finger slid closer and slowly worked down her slit. "Fuck, baby."

She was hot and wet and slippery. How badly he craved to slide into her.

Instead, his finger would do all the work. He dragged some of her liquid heat up to her budding clit and circled it, just as he'd done the prior week. He continued his gentle ministrations, occasionally gathering her essence to help the perfect slide over her tiny bundle of nerves.

She moaned and tilted her hips into his touch.

He loved already how responsive she was. Then he slipped a finger inside her channel, all while caressing her left thigh.

She was perfect. So fucking perfect. Heat radiated off her now, and he knew she had to be close.

After several minutes of his seduction, he stopped. He figured she must be ready to explode about now.

She looked over her shoulder at him and confusion marred her brow.

He didn't stray from his plan. "I want dinner with you." He knew she was used to calling all the shots, but he would prove to her, the rewards would be sweet, if she could temporarily give up some control.

"You asshole," she hissed.

He continued caressing her thighs but didn't give her what she wanted.

"Agree to dinner, next Friday. You can pick the place, and I'll give you exactly what you're aching for."

She glared at him for several beats. She didn't need him, he would bank on that, but Derek would also bet dates with the vibrator were getting old.

"Fine. Dinner."

His lips curled. He would happily finish the job.

His right hand crept back to her center and started his attentions again, wetting her hot button to slide over with just enough pressure.

She moaned.

He didn't stop. He wanted her creaming his fingers.

She gripped her wineglass as her panting accelerated. Her clit twitched, her eyes closed, and she splintered apart beneath him.

He looped an arm around her waist, holding her close as the tremors ripped through her body.

God, she was gorgeous.

After she subsided, he smoothed her skirt straight and took his seat beside her. He waited for her to look at him, then pulled clean his finger from his mouth.

Her mouth gaped and she snapped it closed, giving away an honest reaction.

"That was incredible." Forget the fact that his dick strained in his pants, threatening to bust the zipper.

She lifted her elbows off the counter and refastened her shirt. "That was interesting. Do you need a moment?" she said as she glanced down at his crotch.

"I'll be fine. At least for a little while." He sipped on his whiskey. "I think I've changed my mind. Let's finish our drinks and go grab dinner. I'm starving."

She pursed her lips, no doubt debating allowing him to change the plans on her.

He leaned in closer. "Don't overthink it, Alexis. It's just dinner. You need to eat, right?"

Her facial features softened. "Okay." She finished the last of her wine. "I'd like to go to Adolpho's."

He nearly smiled. "Fine." To use her word.

Chapter Five

LEXI AND DEREK strode in sync toward Adolpho's and she allowed him to open the door for her. She'd picked the place because she'd heard it was good *and* tough to get in without a reservation.

Since he'd agreed so quickly, she was certain Derek wasn't aware of their reputation. Walking to the hostess stand, Lexi was fully prepared to leave once they were told reservations were two months out. She chuckled to herself. She wasn't making it easy for him. Payback for holding her orgasm hostage, so really, it was only fair.

The well-appointed restaurant with black-clothed tables, overhead chandeliers, and patterned carpet smelled like an Italian mamma's kitchen. The scents of basil and oregano lingered in the air, causing Lexi's mouth to water. They stopped short, by the edge of the bar, and Derek turned to her. "Wait right here."

He sauntered confidently down the length of the bar to where a woman, a few inches shorter than Lexi with blonde hair and great boobs, looked up at him. He leaned down to hug her and kiss her cheek. There was an exchange, she nodded, and he made his way back to Lexi.

A pulse of jealousy raced through Lexi, and she hated it. Who was the blonde to him? A previous girlfriend?

Lexi schooled her expression as Derek approached.

"It'll be just a minute." A small smile flashed briefly on his face.

So, did he just sweet-talk his way into getting us a table?

"This place has excellent Italian food," he said. "Have you been here before?"

Of course, he'd been here before, maybe with that blonde. "No, but I'd heard rave reviews so that's why I picked it."

"Good choice."

The blonde came up to them, holding two menus. "Please follow me."

They walked past a few people patiently waiting for a table and Lexi tried not to feel guilty when they were seated along the far wall close to the window. Fine linens and candles graced the table, and as Derek pulled out her heavy chair, she noticed the deep-red velvet cushion. How decadent. It was as soft as it looked.

Lexi slipped off her ridiculous poncho. "So, I take it you've been here before."

"I have." He didn't elaborate; he was doing it

intentionally.

She hid a laugh. She deserved it.

Water was poured as Lexi opened her menu. God, everything sounded so delicious. Her stomach rumbled.

Dinner was one thing, but in the back of Lexi's mind, she wondered what precisely Derek was expecting. Sex certainly, but beyond that, he might be disappointed. She bit the inside of her cheek. The sooner she cleared the air, the better.

The waitress approached.

"Alexis, do you like red wine?" he asked.

"I do."

Derek ordered a bottle of expensive pinot noir that Lexi knew would be tasty with dinner.

She decided on a seafood and pasta dish and laid down the menu. "Okay, so I'll bite. You clearly have connections to this place. Care to elaborate?"

The corners of his perfect lips quirked up. "I work with a man whose wife's family owns this restaurant."

"Ah." She sipped her water and processed what she was feeling. "Let me guess. That blonde is your co-worker's wife?"

"Correct."

Lexi's shoulders relaxed. Thinking about Derek sleeping with another woman had almost made her lose her appetite.

The waitress arrived, opened the bottle of wine, poured some, and then took their dinner orders. Her actions were precise, her voice smooth, and she always attended to Lexi first. She was well-trained.

Derek lifted his wineglass. Lexi mirrored his actions. "To an incredible start of something equally incredible."

She clanked her glass against his; she would toast to sex anytime.

"Have you done that before?" she asked, referring to the escapade at the bar.

He met her gaze and a small sparkle shown in the dim light. "No."

Every woman liked to think they were special in some form or fashion. Lexi was no different. Even though this relationship would be sex only, that didn't mean she couldn't occasionally feel like a queen.

"So, this is what I'm thinking—sex, and only sex."

He tipped his head, his expression returned to neutral. "I'm not allowed to feed you?"

She had to be careful. She didn't want to string him along. "Fine. Some food."

"Okay." He sipped from his wineglass. "Are we going over the rules?"

Her mouth twitched. "Yes, I suppose we are."

"Lay it on me. What do you want?"

She had a once-in-lifetime opportunity to create the perfect relationship—for lack of a better word—with a man. She got to define the boundaries and take what she wanted without risking her heart. She'd been burned in the past.

She held up her finger, adding a digit for each of her

requirements. "Sex plus food. Weekends only. And don't fall in love with me."

His watch-face reflected the candle in the center of the table as he scratched his chin. He didn't interrupt or argue.

Lexi continued, "No dating or sleeping with anyone else. I won't go there." She watched his expression for any reaction that told her he couldn't accept the terms.

"Agreed."

So far so good. "Condoms every time, unless you show proof that you're clean. I'm clean and on the pill."

He sucked in a breath of air.

Good, she'd surprised him. Ha! But really, she was not a fan of condoms though they were a necessary evil.

"Anything else?" He rested his forearm on the table.

"No whips and chains or threesomes. Oh, and no anal. That is simply not pleasurable." She rolled her eyes thinking how Dillion had tried that crap on her. Anal was definitely a one-sided adventure, and Lexi was out. Period.

To Derek's credit, his deep hazel eyes were trained on her the entire time. He didn't flinch or look around at whoever might overhear her.

"Is that it?" He pushed away the knife and spoon in front of him.

Lexi took another delicious sip of wine. *This stuff is going down like Kool-Aid.* She gave a single nod.

"Okay, my turn."

She nodded again. That was fair.

"Blindfolds, when I feel like it. No anal, fine, but that probably means you were with the wrong man."

That was the understatement of the year, and the year was only half over.

He leaned across the table closer toward her, drawing her in with his voice. "I get all of your fantasies. I get you anywhere and everywhere I want."

Her jaw dropped. *Anywhere and everywhere?* Could she handle that? The bar stuff might have been just a little taste of what Derek was capable of.

"And if I say no?"

He straightened and reached for his wine. "That's fine. But this restaurant will be the last time I see you."

Whoa! He was serious.

Shit! What to do? How far could he take it? She had to find out. She hadn't had sex with him yet, but somehow knew he would be amazing. She wasn't ready to throw in the towel. Leaving at some future time was always an option, if necessary.

"Okay." She forced her chin high and held his gaze. "I agree."

Derek lifted his glass to hers, and they clinked in harmony. "We have a deal." He reached into his back pocket for his wallet and retrieved a business card. He slid it across the table and waited for her.

She rifled through her purse and dug out her card, setting it before him.

He examined the card in the candlelight. "That explains your amazing shoes."

She smiled. "Thank you."

The waitress served their meals. Lexi enjoyed her pasta as they chatted about surface stuff.

"When did you open AK Designs?"

"Ten years ago." This was a safe enough topic, but she wanted to know about him too. "I have four stores and the fifth opens in Forest Ridge next month."

"How did you get started?"

"My friend, Rachel, talked me into taking fashion design with her our senior year in high school. Rachel had a knack for sewing, and I had an interest in fashion, especially shoes."

"Following your dream and making it a reality." His smile held approval. "Do you create everything?"

"I started out designing, but now I don't have as much time, so I've hired other creative people to help." Well, creative people after she hired Raffaele's replacement.

"Congratulations."

The corners of her lips curved upward. "Thank you. And what about you," she glanced at his card again, standard corporate America-issued, "Mr. CFO?"

Derek thought about how best to answer her question. He had a few different ways to respond. Given how Alexis was dead-set on keeping this purely physical, she likely wouldn't appreciate his life's story. On the other hand, giving her a peek at Derek the man might gain some brownie points from this sassy, hard-as-nails woman.

"I've been with Vigers for eight years, gaining several promotions along the way. I've worked for everything in my life since my senior year in college." He wouldn't get into all the gory details. "My parents divorced when I was twelve. My favorite sport is basketball. And I prefer dogs to cats. If I didn't work so much, I'd have a dog named Rufus."

Her blue eyes twinkled. "You said you weren't married, but have you ever been?"

"Nope. You?" He tore off a piece of the focaccia bread and dunked it in olive oil.

"Nope, and I've no intention to walk down the aisle."

Derek saw the subtle change in her expression on the topic of marriage. Clearly, she'd been wronged in this department. Nevertheless, he wanted to keep things upbeat, so he asked, "Alexis, are you a dog person or a cat person? Think carefully."

She chewed a bite of her pasta, then swallowed, smiling. "You can call me Lexi. And I'm a dog person. If I had a dog, she'd be named Bella."

He grinned.

Good. He'd known she would be a tough nut to crack, but he'd faced tougher obstacles in his life and wouldn't be defeated. Patience would be the key to earning Lexi's trust. He couldn't say why but a strictly sexual relationship didn't sit well with Derek, not when he had a feeling there could be so much more.

The waitress checked on them again, making sure dinner ran smoothly without being overbearing. He would tell Liam that Adolpho's was top of the line from service to food.

Lexi had no doubt chosen this restaurant as part of her vetting process. The men who failed her tests probably hadn't even known what hit them. Just—bam!—like that, they were out.

What Derek didn't understand was why the fuck she was single. Lexi was a catch—gorgeous, smart, successful, and sexy. The combination was unbeatable. Surely, there had been at least one man along the way who had met her high standards.

Her reaction to the marriage topic alerted him to some crevasses in the road when it came to men, and perhaps that was why she kept herself so guarded. Derek would be enduring. A confident woman had the makings of happily ever after in his mind.

Witnessing everything his parents had gone through, his mother on her fourth marriage... Uh-uh, no sir. Derek was sure this was why he'd stayed a bachelor for so long. He believed in the sacrament too much to treat it lightly.

He hadn't talked to his father in years. And his poor mom, on her fourth marriage searching for something she needed to give herself, but she couldn't see that. Thanks to Renee, his mentor, he understood what a loving relationship could be, and now that his career was sorted, well, he might have met Lexi at the perfect time.

They wrapped up dinner, and he drove her back to Bogart's. She pointed out where her car was parked—a luxury import, no less. It suited her.

She opened the door and glanced back when he didn't move. "Your place or mine?"

He met her gaze, wanting to go there, but he didn't budge. The sacrifice now would be worth it in the long game.

She lifted an eyebrow and settled back into her seat.

"Another night. I want you to sleep on our new arrangement. I don't want you to regret it in the morning. I want to make sure you're all in. But know this, Alexis." He gripped her hand and kissed her soft palm and delicate wrist. "This won't be a one-night stand. If I have you once, I'll want to fuck you again. I will make it good for you because it will always be about maximum pleasure. Are you all right with that?"

Lexi visibly swallowed, then shrugged and pulled free from his grasp. "Fine. I'll sleep on it. But I won't be waiting for your call." She gave him one of her sassy smiles and rose from the car, pushing the door closed behind her, not looking back.

Hot damn! She was a pistol.

Derek sat in his car, making sure she drove off safely, adjusting his pants for his growing erection. He had to have her. He *would* have her. All of her—including her heart.

Chapter Six

MONDAY MORNING, TONIA walked through the open door of Lexi's office. Lexi couldn't even see her assistant's face because of the insane bouquet of flowers in her hands.

"Lexi, these just arrived for you." Tonia's voice pitched high with excitement. "You must have had a great weekend."

She cleared a space on her desk for Tonia to set down the glass vase. "Well, these are pretty." Lexi knew in her heart who'd sent them. No note necessary. She'd half-expected Derek to do something over-the-top. She admired the mass of fresh stems, from roses to lilies.

"And this came with it." Tonia handed her an envelope with *Alexis King* handwritten across the front.

"Thanks."

Tonia smiled and retreated to the outer office.

Lexi inhaled the floral arrangement before opening the envelope. The first thing catching her eye was a full medical report of sexually transmitted diseases, performed the prior day. *Sunday.* Some that were listed she'd never heard of before—all negative.

Next, she slipped out a handwritten note—*This is me calling. Have dinner with me Friday night.*

She grinned at his audacity. Okay, this is a good first step.

Lexi dug in her purse to retrieve his business card. She typed out a text.

Thank you for the flowers. I also appreciate the report. You didn't waste a minute, did you?

She smirked and waited only a moment for his reply.

I know what I want. Does that mean you'll have dinner—and dessert—with me?

Oh yes, dessert sounded divine.

Yes.

She sent him her address, then put her phone away. She had a busy day, a busy week, going through the portfolios starting to come in, interviewing, and sketching some new designs. She couldn't be distracted by some gorgeous man who had great fingers and probably other great things too.

Mmm.

God, was she that crazy? She could admit to being a risk-taker, but was this taking it too far—to allow a complete stranger free reign over her body?

Body, fine. Heart, no freakin' way. Been there, done that. Been burned by not just her asshole stepfather but also by cheating boyfriends.

One question continued to roll around in her head—where did Derek come from?

Seriously. Men didn't just drop out of thin air, giving insane offers of sexual satisfaction with the skillset to follow through. Not to mention his good looks, confidence, and charisma. Real confidence, not the false bravado she'd seen a million and one times.

She was too busy to overthink it. She'd had physical relationships that never turned into anything serious, which suited Lexi just fine.

So, spending more than a few minutes ruminating over a man could really be considered excessive. *So stop it!*

Before she could dive into her inbox, her office phone rang. *Rachel* splashed across the screen.

"Hey, chica."

"Hey. Guess what? Hunter is taking the kids to an Astros game Wednesday night. He asked if I wanted to go, but I thought we could have some girl-time instead. Are you free?"

The ladies had a ritual of getting together weekly for dinner, and rarely did they miss it.

"That sounds great. Want to go out, or stay in? My place, or your place?" Time with her best friend was exactly what Lexi needed. Rachel gave great advice.

"Stay in—my house. Come early and we'll have a few drinks on the back patio. I'll make a chef salad since the kids hate it."

Ah, yes, even better. They chatted a bit more and then

wrapped up the conversation. They'd have plenty of time Wednesday night for Lexi to share everything. And boy, Rachel would need a drink or two once she heard what Lexi had to tell her.

~

Lexi rang Rachel's front doorbell. Before Hunter had moved in, she'd just ring and open the door herself but she didn't feel comfortable doing that now; she didn't want to disturb the happy couple's privacy.

The door opened and Lexi glanced down. Her two favorite munchkins, Violet and Ethan, stood before her, waving giant foam fingers.

"Aunt Lexi!" They practically tackled her with their hugs.

"Hi, guys." She ushered them across the threshold to the foyer. "I thought you'd be at the game already."

"We're leaving right now." A harried Hunter strode toward the door but paused to kiss her cheek. "Rach is in the kitchen. You two have fun tonight."

"Thanks. You guys too." Lexi leaned down and planted smooches on the tops of the kids' heads.

The door closed behind them as the trio laughingly left to cheer on the Astros. Hunter made an amazing dad and genuinely loved the kids.

Lexi found Rachel squatted down with her head in a cabinet, comfy in her cutoffs, flip-flops, and her blonde hair in a high ponytail. "Uh, what's goin' on?"

Rachel sat back on her haunches. "Hey. I'm looking for my Bundt pan. I thought I'd make a cake." She rose. "Never mind. Maybe next time." She pulled out two stemmed glasses and rested them on the counter in front of Lexi, then retrieved the white wine from the fridge. "You pour. Do you even want cake?"

Lexi laughed. "No." She filled the glasses to the top. "So, what's new? How's work going?" Rachel was the executive assistant to the CEO of Blazer Electronic. She'd been there for several years and was good at her job.

"Same ol', same ol'. Come on."

Lexi followed her to the back patio of the house. It was an exceptional view of the lake just beyond their backyard, so picturesque and peaceful. They drained their first round over basic chit-chat.

As Rachel refilled their wineglasses, Lexi decided now was a good time to fill her in on her latest escapade.

"So." She cleared her throat. "Remember that surprising thing that happened to you on your fortieth when we took you to the strip club?"

Rachel's cheeks tinted pink at the recollection of the male dancers taking a few liberties with her on stage that night. "Yeah."

"Well, I had an equally surprising event happen recently."

"Oh? Do tell." Rach bent her knees and pulled her legs

onto the chair.

Lexi licked her lips, wondering how much detail she should reveal, but Rachel already knew Lexi was the wild one. "I went to Bogart's after work two Fridays ago."

Rachel glanced off to the side, searching her memory. "Ah, yes. The day you found out about Raffaele."

"Uhh, don't remind me. Anyway, I was drinking my bourbon and 7Up when a man sorta just appeared beside me. He was handsome, for sure, but that doesn't always mean much."

"True." Rachel took a healthy sip.

"So, he started talking to me, and frankly I just wanted to be left alone, but he was witty," she shrugged a shoulder, "so I guess I was a bit intrigued. And he also...challenged me."

"Challenged you?" Rachel parroted.

"He said things like, I was probably stressed out and that's why I was at the bar. That work was monotonous, and life had become boring."

"That was bold."

"Yup, and although it wasn't a hundred percent accurate, it certainly got my attention. Anyway, he said I was probably looking for a challenge to stir things up." She waited for Rachel to finish her swallow. "And he proceeded to offer to make me come right there in the bar, without touching my skin."

Her best friend's eyes rounded to saucers. "Holy cow, Lexi."

"I know."

"And what did you tell him?"

Lexi traced the stem of her wineglass. "What could I say?" Half-smiling, half wincing, she said, "I mean, I can't back down from a challenge."

"No way." Rachel chuckled. "That is far more explicit than what I had at the strip club."

Lexi knew that to be true. Rachel probably would have thrown her drink in Derek's face if she were in Lexi's shoes.

"So how was it?" Rachel asked, grinning.

"Good." So freakin' hot that Lexi's muscles clenched at the memory. "But Friday it was even better."

Rachel leaned forward and slapped her thigh. "Friday? You saw him again?"

Lexi bit down on her lip and nodded. "It was sorta part of the deal. Since he made me come, he technically won the challenge. So, I had to show up again a week later. Without panties on."

"Oh my God, Lex." Rachel fanned her face with her napkin.

"Rach, it was so hot, and now we have a date this Friday." *Date* was a loosely defined term for her.

"So, not your typical category candidate, I take it?"

"Nope. I might need to start a new category. Strictly for men who know how to please." She gave an exuberant smile.

Rachel exhaled and lifted her glass in a toast. "Well, good for you."

"We'll see."

"Look, you haven't dated anyone in quite a while. This will be great for you. And who knows, maybe you've found The One."

Lexi's heart skipped a beat and she forced in a breath. "Um, I don't know about that."

Rachel knew all the sordid details of the "spectacular" men Lexi'd had in her life and waved her hand dismissively. "Doesn't matter! Give it time and see where it goes. It sounds like it's off to a fabulous start." She grinned and rose to bring out the garden salad for dinner.

Alexis *really* didn't want the relationship-thing. She'd been burned too often to count. But she realized what she'd been missing: great sex. Sex was the solution to fixing all of her woes. Why hadn't she thought of this sooner?

Sure, there had been men—some good, some not so good. She could already tell Derek was on a whole other level. She could totally ride this train for a while, sow her sexual oats, clear her head, and get back in the game, particularly as it related to AK. She probably would have seen the signs with Raffaele sooner if she hadn't been so out of tune with her needs.

As long as Derek didn't expect happily ever after, they were in amazing shape for fun times.

Rachel tended to see relationships these days through rose-colored glasses because she was engaged to be married and had found her happily ever after. That wasn't in the cards for Lexi, but she was okay with that.

~

Derek parked in front of Lexi's apartment building Friday evening. She lived in a secure complex with lots of modern touches, lush landscaping, and covered parking. It made Derek feel a million times more comfortable knowing the place had a guard on duty twenty-four-seven.

He rang the bell. He'd half-expected her to text him to say she'd meet him at the curb. There was no way he'd put up with that—but she'd proved him wrong.

She answered the door wearing a black, fitted sheath and strappy black high heels. Her hair and makeup were perfect. Not that she needed much of anything—she was truly beautiful.

"Hello." Lexi stepped back to let him inside her personal space.

"Hi." He leaned down and kissed her cheek before she could object, then presented her with a bouquet of flowers.

"More flowers." The words were droll but the tone, pleased.

"Sure. Now you have some for home and some for work." He grinned and turned to check out her place.

Like her luxury car, it suited her—wood floors, marble tile fireplace surround, moldings around the windows and at the high ceiling, but with splashes of color: a throw on the sofa, the pillows, the area rug, linen drapes on the windows.

It was high-end without being ostentatious.

"Nice apartment."

"Thanks," she called from the kitchen as she filled a vase with water for the flowers. "It's not too far from my office, which is the best perk."

After getting her card, he'd done a little research on Alexis King. He wanted to learn all he could about this woman who was so guarded. *Any* information was helpful, including the address of where she worked.

She slung her red designer bag over her shoulder and approached him. "Ready when you are."

"Great." He held open the door for her.

"Where are we going?"

He wanted to say *your bedroom* and turn them both around, but that wasn't the makings of a relationship. Sex was a great springboard, not a foundation. He would get to know her, and then *she* would get to know how much she wanted him in her life, not just in her bed.

"I was thinking Chez Jay. They have a new chef I've heard good things about."

She glanced up at him over her sunglasses. "You don't know the owners?"

He grinned. "Nope, not this time."

They arrived at the restaurant and Derek was only too happy to have Lexi on his arm. Well, not literally. He knew she would not appreciate having her arm looped around his—

that was a move "dating couples" did, and they were not dating, in Lexi's eyes.

Derek, self-aware, was the classic lifetime bachelor. He'd dated plenty of women, each and every time making it clear he wasn't interested in marriage. They had all agreed though some had left when they were ready to settle down. Some—oh gees—had hoped to change his mind. His mind wouldn't be changed, and they'd learned the hard way. He was happy with his decision. Replicating the life of his parents didn't appeal to Derek in the least.

That said, he was smart enough to realize when the world shifts around you, you recognize it and embrace it. That shift was called Alexis King.

His hand rested on her lower back as he guided her inside and then to their table where he pulled out her chair. It would start slow, but the small exposures to "regular" relationship stuff was going to be key in propelling this relationship forward.

They'd agreed on committed sex; he didn't mention a long-term relationship. He couldn't risk scaring her off. But slowly, he would tear down those walls she'd built around herself and let the real Lexi out.

Chapter Seven

DEREK ORDERED CAKEBREAD Reserve Chardonnay with dinner. Lexi adored Cakebread. She didn't often have it because of the price tag, so this was a treat.

They chatted over dinner about work—his and hers. Now that she knew him better, Lexi told him about the fiasco with Rafaelle and why she'd been at Bogart's that fateful Friday night.

"So, I suppose you fired him," Derek asked before slipping a bite of sea bass into his mouth.

Derek had a great mouth—full and sensual. They hadn't kissed yet. This was the third time they'd been together and...he was doing a helluva job of keeping her guessing.

"Absolutely. Then I confronted the president, Henry Bumpass. Flew to Kansas City and told him to stay away from my company." She tasted her scallops. Divine.

Derek looked up from his dinner plate, his mouth agape. "No shit."

"No shit." Lexi was proud of herself. No one was going

to toy with her or her company like that. "I think he still has a chip on his shoulder because I interviewed a candidate at the same time as him. But I won."

Derek set down his fork and leaned back, holding her gaze the entire time. "Damn, that's impressive. I should have ordered champagne so we can celebrate. You're a helluva warrior."

She grinned. She couldn't say why, but hearing the pride in his voice made her warm inside. She was probably reading too much into it.

"Anyway, I'm interviewing for a new designer now."

"How's that going?"

"Fine overall. Designing shoes has a different perspective to it, so getting someone who can design apparel, for example, is only half my battle. But I have some good prospects. In the meantime, I've dusted off my sketch pad."

"Oh? I thought you didn't have time for that."

Derek didn't miss much. "I really don't, but we gotta do what we gotta do." Lexi sighed internally. "And how are things in your world?" She had to change the subject. She didn't want to think about falling into her old ways of doing too much and losing her life balance.

"Good. Issues are cropping up that seem to be more of a focus than ever before. So, some days are a bit challenging."

I know about those days.

She rested her knife and fork across her empty plate and lifted her wineglass. "Like what? Anything you can talk about?" Lexi was quickly learning that Derek was easy to talk to.

"Uh-huh. Data security is a big concern right now. We're seeing more cyber-attacks in the business world. The government will do its part, we hope, against attacks from other countries, namely Russia and China, right? But ultimately our customers will come to *us* looking for the best security they can get."

"Wow. So, what can you do?"

"As fast as technology changes, we need to be able to implement just as fast a means to stay ahead of the curve. It also takes talent—the best and the brightest." He said it matter-of-factly, no big deal, but Lexi had the feeling that things like this made Derek's job very stressful.

"And to think, I thought you were just a bean counter," she said with a teasing tone.

He laughed. "Not anymore. The role of CFO has definitely changed over the years. It has more responsibility when it comes to operations than ever before."

Derek was smart and that impressed Lexi. She'd had a sense of it during their first meeting, as he'd called her out on her need for more.

"How about we get outta here?" he asked.

"Okay," she countered, "but now I get to see your place." Lexi couldn't wait to examine his lair as he'd perused hers.

"That's fair."

Derek pulled his car into the parking garage beneath his tall, modern condominium building, and Lexi thought it seemed like glass for miles. He lived outside of Houston in Baybrook, an exclusive little town because of its premium location near the bay.

He held Lexi's hand leading her to the elevator, and she let him. She didn't need a show of affection, but it was a minor concession, so she'd give in. So far, he'd treated her with the ultimate respect. It was a turn on.

He held open the door to his condo for her to walk through.

Holy fuck!

The place was huge, open, and modern. Sleek cement floors, pristine white cabinets with marble quartz countertops, a low L-shaped sectional sofa, and an entire wall of windows facing the bay. Since it was dark outside, Lexi couldn't see the ocean, but she could imagine the incredible view.

She pivoted back to his voice, following it to the kitchen. "You have a great place here, Derek."

The mortgage would be out of this world.

"Thanks. I love it, although I don't spend as much time here as I'd really like."

She'd suspected that. For one, he had an A-type personality like her, work hard and play hard. And two, there wasn't a single personal item in the place. No photos of friends or family.

Maybe that was one reason why he was so into her—like attracts like.

"I'll give you the nickel-tour." Derek walked around the counter, and Lexi couldn't help but admire his firm backside. She wanted to reach out and squeeze his ass through his slacks.

She cleared her throat and yanked her gaze up just as he turned toward her.

"Can I get you something to drink?"

"Water, please."

He lifted the water pitcher from the fridge and filled two glasses. "This is really just two rooms—the great room and the bedroom. Anywhere in the condo you can see the water, well, in the light." Derek's smile made her insides flutter.

She strolled through the kitchen—the chef's six-burner range hardly looked used. Another thing they had in common.

He led her to the bedroom, and she followed, glass in hand. She nearly tripped over herself passing through the doorway.

Derek flipped on a table lamp, but she could already see how fantastic the expansive room was. In the middle sat a high, black, four-poster, king-sized bed made of metal, situated to face the water and another entire wall of glass. Under the bed was a large plush solid white area rug, and the only other furniture was one nightstand and a dresser, which was pushed against the front wall. The bed was center stage.

The two doors she surmised went to the bathroom and the closet.

"Wow," she breathed out. "You have impeccable taste."

"Thanks."

She strode to the window, hoping to get a glimpse of anything through the darkness. The water would be incredible.

He walked up behind her and stroked his hands over her upper arms. "You'll have to come back during the day. It's a nice view, especially when no big ships disrupt it."

"Mmhm."

He planted a small kiss on the side of her neck. She couldn't move, his warm lips felt too damn good against her skin. She craved a kiss from him.

Lexi tasted divine, and he couldn't wait to have more. "I've been thinking about fucking you all damn week," he whispered against her neck. That wasn't *entirely* true. He'd been thinking about *her*, but he couldn't say that because she'd read into it too much and likely get spooked.

"Mmm."

He unzipped the back of her dress and exposed a few more inches of delicious skin to kiss and lick. He pushed her hair aside. "I'd wake up hard with images of you coming on my fingers at the bar and imagine what it would be like if it were my tongue instead."

She moaned, and he slipped the dress off her shoulders,

letting it puddle around her feet.

He bent down. "Turn around and step out, Alexis."

She spun around to face him, wearing only a black bra, matching thong, and her sexy high heels. He stepped back to take in the sight, quite sure she would see the wood he was sporting beneath his trousers.

He closed the gap and cupped her jaw. "You are sexy as fuck, Alexis." He leaned down to claim her lush lips. Something else he'd been dreaming about: their first kiss.

She opened for him and met his tongue with equal voracity. Her hands made fast work of his button-down shirt and pushed it off his shoulders.

They broke the kiss, her sweet breath lightly panting over his mouth.

She leaned back and stroked his chest with her delicate hands. "You're a gym rat."

He grinned at the phrase. "I am."

"I knew it." She leaned in to kiss and lick his chest, and at the same time, began loosening his pants.

He flicked off her bra, letting it fall to the floor, just as she pushed his pants and briefs over his hips.

In a flash, she bent to her knees and took him in her fist and her mouth.

"Fuuck, Alexis."

Her mouth was insane wrapped around him.

He tightened his muscles to stave off the impending orgasm. He let her continue for a few brief moments until he hauled her upright. His mouth covered hers as he pushed her against the glass.

He lifted her hands over her head and pinned them with one of his. His mouth moved from her lips to her gorgeous, pointed nipples, sucking and toying with them.

"Unh!" She arched into his mouth like a jolt.

He could tell she was just as ready to explode as he was—still keeping her pinned to the glass wall, he slid down her torso to her covered mound. He yanked down her panties a few inches to get to his prize.

"Fuck," she moaned when he dragged his finger through her warm, slick center.

"I will. But first, I want you coming." He held her gaze as he tugged her panties just an inch or two more. "Now, spread your legs."

She barely moved.

"More, Alexis. I don't care about your panties. I'll buy you dozens." He stroked her lips and gently teased her clit. Her panting increased.

She widened her stance, stretching the fabric to the max.

He loved seeing her debauched and sexy as fuck stretched out before him for the taking. She was all his for the night. Really the only question was how many times he could make her come before dawn.

His mouth reclaimed a hardened nipple as his finger rolled over and around her clit.

She mewled.

"So fucking wet, Alexis." He toyed and played, bringing her to the edge and backing down. He didn't keep her in agony long. He thrust two fingers inside her channel as his thumb circled her clit, adding just enough pressure.

She cried out as her hips writhed against his hand.

He gave her just enough time to calm down, but before she opened her eyes, he'd swung her around to the bed. He gently tossed her face-down over his high bed, yanked free her panties with a tug of his hands, and dove his cock into her.

"Fuck," he yelled.

She felt like homecoming. Heaven and homecoming. He already knew; he would do anything for this woman.

He thrust through her panting and whispered into her neck as his hand clamped down on her hair, immobilizing her head. "This pussy is mine, Alexis." All of her was his, she just wouldn't admit it. Yet.

He was rough but somehow knew that was exactly what she needed.

She groaned as he thrust, claiming every possible inch her pussy would allow until he could hold on no longer. He spurt out his seed, filling her up. First fuck of the last woman he might ever have in his life. The thought made him smile.

He gently eased out of her and laid to the side, resisting the urge to pull her into him.

Her breath quieted when she spoke, "You definitely owe

me new panties."

Good, he would keep these.

"You're right. Do you want to go out now?"

She opened her eyes, giving him an *are you crazy* look. "Assuming anything would be open, I'm sure that would be great—showing up, smelling freshly fucked."

He wiggled his brows. "I wouldn't care."

"I don't doubt it." But in the dim light, he noticed her mouth curving with humor.

Slowly but surely, he would win her over.

Chapter Eight

LEXI'D HAD A productive week, and she was feeling good. Brea's new wedge sandal in five colors had great sales so far for the summer. Roseanne had returned from maternity leave so the backlog of price-promotion reporting could be brought up to date. And the copy for the new fall lineup looked fabulous.

She wouldn't think about the designing she felt compelled to do to relieve the burden on Brea. But damn, if she could just find a decent designer, one who would fit well in the AK culture...

Since it was Saturday, she could work *or* take some time and do something for herself.

Derek popped in her head, and she couldn't help but smile. They'd seen each other last night and the previous weekend and fucked several times Friday, Saturday, *and* Sunday. Sometimes at his place, sometimes at hers. He'd asked her to spend the night one time, but that was not gonna work.

But all that delicious sex, sweet baby Jesus. She could get addicted to that.

As long as you don't get addicted to him.

Before she could scold herself any further, an idea darted to the forefront.

She threw back the covers and headed to the bathroom. After brushing her teeth, she slipped on shorts and a T-shirt, and yanked on her running shoes. She grabbed her baseball hat and purse to make her way to her favorite coffee shop. After that, she'd go to the gym, but after a morning-coffee-drop off as a thank you to Derek.

The barista knew her order by the sight of Lexi's face.

"Hi," the barista said. Lexi pegged her to be in her twenties with lots of energy. "The usual?"

"Yes, but make it two." Derek liked strong black coffee, but she'd introduce him to a cappuccino—an espresso shot with foam. He'd introduced her to new things, and that had turned out great. Lexi chuckled to herself.

It was barely seven in the morning, but this would wake him up. She added muffins for breakfast to the order.

Loading the goodies into her car, she mentally searched for directions to where he lived—she didn't have his address for her GPS. She drove through light traffic—praise the heavens—and arrived at Derek's in Baybrook in under twenty minutes.

The doorman rose from his desk. "Hello. May I help you?"

She searched his chest and read off his name tag. "Good morning, Terrence. I'm here to see Derek Hollister." She flashed the coffees. "Could you tell me what floor he's on?"

"He's not there, ma'am."

That stopped Lexi cold in her tracks. Her breath stalled. She met Terrence's eyes.

Fuck! Was he seeing someone else? We agreed. The shithead.

"No?"

"No, ma'am. He's at the basement level. In the gym."

She exhaled in relief. "Oh, okay. I'll head that way. I didn't think he'd be up this early."

"Yes, ma'am." Terrence nodded and sat back down at his station in the lobby.

She took the short elevator ride, turned the corner, and quickly spied the large gym. *Wow!*

The wall of glass showcased the cardio machines, weight machines, free weights, mats for stretching—they had everything. Derek lifted a barbell over his head. She had no idea how much weight was on there, but it looked heavy. He was handling it, no problem.

Lexi realized that he was the only one in the gym. As he lowered the weight, she opened the door and entered. Her confidence was momentarily shaken with her interaction with Terrence, but it had been a false alarm. They'd agreed to the rules; that shouldn't be difficult to keep.

He caught her reflection in the mirror and turned

around to meet her gaze.

"I come bearing breakfast."

His mouth quirked as he tracked her moving closer toward him. He set down the barbell. "You're actually dressed to work out."

"I am. I thought I'd drop by for coffee, then head to my gym. I rarely get to work out as much as I'd like."

He stepped closer and into her personal space. Cupping her cheeks, he leaned down and claimed her lips. The kiss was deep and consuming, and with her hands full, she could do nothing but stand there and take every delicious bit of what this man laid on her.

His masculine scent filled the air around them, stealing her ability to think clearly.

He broke their heated connection. "What have ya got there?"

She was nearly breathless with his unexpected tongue kiss. "Cappuccino."

He lifted her hand, picked up the cup from the carrier, and sipped. "Not bad. Something different."

"That's what I was thinking. Something a little different."

"Yes, well, the coffee can wait. I want something a little different too." His husky voice told her just what he had in mind.

He took the packages from her hands and walked them to the far side of the gym, setting them on a table that held water and hand towels. He turned around, his erection evident in his charcoal nylon shorts. "Come here, Alexis."

She edged back. "Oh, no, Derek. Anyone could come down here and see us." The words left her mouth, and at the same time, moisture gathered at her sex. "Let's go upstairs to your condo."

His steps covered the floor in a split second. She tried to make it to the door, but she was too slow. He looped an arm around her waist, hauling her flush against his solid body. "Anytime. Anywhere." He tipped her head back with his free hand and licked up the side of her neck. "I don't care about the risk. I want to fuck you until you scream."

She nearly melted into him. Her nipples peaked as he continued kissing her neck, his hand skimming down her front.

He gently tugged at her shorts, lowering them an inch, then he yanked her T-shirt overhead. His lips returned to hers. He whispered, "Are you getting wet, my sweet?"

His hand glossed over her breasts to the waistband of her nylon running shorts. His hand slipped inside.

They were two feet from the door and she was paralyzed to stop him. She ached for him more than she worried about being caught. Of course, she *should* worry, but fuck it, she wanted Derek more than she'd ever wanted a man. Well, *parts* of her wanted him.

And then he slid his finger through her slit. "Oh, that's my girl."

She'd grown wet and eager. She glanced over her shoulder toward the bank of elevators. No one there.

But before she could grasp what was going on, he'd lifted her up and laid her on a nearby padded bench. Then with two hands on her shorts, he tugged. Her shorts flew down her legs, hooking onto one gym shoe. She hadn't worn panties; it wasn't necessary with the self-liner of her shorts.

"Oh God." She tried to reach for the shorts, but it was useless. Derek lowered his body and lay claim to her pussy in no-time flat.

"Ah," she called out. *Oh God, his mouth.*

His hands pushed apart her legs, giving him complete access.

The room spun, or maybe it was just her head. He made love to her sex in the most amazing way, conquering every square inch. The scruff on his face titillated her nether lips. His hand reached up to her sports bra, lifting it over her breasts, baring them to the room. Or anyone who might come downstairs. Effectively, she was naked.

He twisted and pulled on her nipples, sending delightful rays of electricity down to her eager pussy.

She writhed and moaned, her hands gripping his head. A little twitch fluttered through her sex.

"That's right, precious," he said in a low tone.

"I don't like being called Precious," she tossed back at him. Asshole Dillion had called her that one too many times.

He raised his head, his lips glistening. "Oh, I wasn't

referring to you." Then, with both hands on her legs, he skimmed up and down her inner thighs.

She gasped when he reached the apex, a highly sensitive area. So anxious for release.

His long fingers danced over her nether lips. "I was referring to this—so warm, wet, and delicate." He stroked the area gently, barely making contact with her clit. "That's not you at all, is it? You're more determined, focused, and demanding, right?"

"And you think," her panting came quicker now, "you'll be the one to crack my shell."

"Nope, wouldn't dream of it." He sucked in one nipple and toyed with it. "I just want the chance to slip underneath it occasionally. A chance for you to set your armor aside long enough to trust me with your raw, vulnerable self." His hot breath blew gently over her face.

Ah, wishful thinking. But then Derek dove two fingers into her wet channel, and all thought was once again lost.

He leaned back down, circling his tongue over her swollen clit.

A movement came into her peripheral vision. Was someone in the hall? She would have to arch her neck way back, but with Derek doing that delicious movement with his tongue—oh hell—the dam of lust and passion broke free, and her orgasm detonated. Electric currents raced to every corner of her body, causing her to cry out.

He stood, pulling off his shorts, and at the same time he

dove into her mouth, he dove into her. His kiss drowned out her scream. Her arms and legs wrapped around him, rocking with him, as he pummeled her like he was born to please her.

She had no idea if the audience was still there, she wanted Derek. The way he licked her, kissed her, fucked her, she didn't give a rat's ass who watched. She was on Cloud Nine, and nothing would take that away.

Derek stole a peek while his lips were still consuming Lexi's. A brown-haired guy, about six-foot, stood just at the corner of the elevators with a clear view into the gym. Derek recognized him as a tenant but didn't know his name.

The man didn't do anything ridiculous, like whip out a camera. Instead, he just watched as Derek licked Lexi's luscious pussy, as she screamed out her orgasm, and as he dove into her, claiming her. Imprinting himself on her so she would never forget how good it felt being with him. How she would want only him for the rest of her life. How she'd know forevermore that she was his.

Derek pumped several more times, his orgasm cataclysmic, maybe because he knew he had an audience.

Fuck, he didn't want to pull out of her.

She opened her glassy eyes, panting and staring up at him. "Wow."

He grinned and could see the figure by the elevators was gone. Derek slipped out of Lexi. "Wait here."

He retrieved a towel and returned to see Lexi's bra back

in position and her legs closed, toes hanging off the edge of the bench. The expression of passion was slowly being replaced with shock.

He wiped her gingerly and wove her foot through her blue shorts. "I see that look. Don't spend one single second overthinking this."

"I think someone saw us." She worried her bottom lip.

"It doesn't matter."

Her eyes rounded and she sat up quickly. "Someone did?"

"He sure did." Derek gripped her chin gently. "It was hot. He's probably upstairs jackin' off to the image of your gorgeous body spread out for my taking."

Color rose in her cheeks.

He took her hand and splayed it over his growing dick. "It would happen to me."

The corner of her lip lifted.

"Now take your coffee and get on with your day. Or stay here and I'll continue my *work out* on your naked body."

She swallowed, then jumped up, grabbed her warm drink, and headed for the door.

"And Alexis."

She angled back to meet his gaze in the mirror, hand on the door handle.

"This doesn't change anything. I'll still be over tonight to fuck you." He leaned down, lifting the bar to finish his overhead presses.

He heard the glass door swish closed.

A thought popped into his head. He started chuckling. The chuckling grew, and he became breathless. He set down the weight bar and glanced up at the camera mounted in the upper east corner he'd completely forgotten about.

He snorted. "You're welcome, Terrence." The man couldn't hear him, but probably read the words coming out of his mouth.

Chapter Nine

LEXI STARED AT her computer screen in her office.

Something was off.

Gregory had just left her office after reviewing the financials from the last fiscal year and then tweaking the budget for this year.

There were no surprises in the budget. Since that had been created months ago, it was merely a matter of revising it for additional online marketing she wanted to try, which started the following month: July. And, of course, she kept the line item for a designer. She might revise it if she hired two part-timers instead.

Lexi had decided when she opened her company ten years ago in June to use that as her fiscal year. She wouldn't change it to the calendar year—and she was still good with that.

What bothered her were the numbers for last fiscal year's sales. She mentally accounted for the snafu with Raffaele, but it still didn't sit right.

She let out a heavy sigh. In thirty minutes, she was supposed to meet Derek for dinner, then probably a trip back to his place, so she needed to wrap it up. With Houston traffic, there was a good probability she'd already be late.

With rare exception did Derek and Alexis meet during the week. She had talked about being too busy, so he accepted that. For now. But he'd convinced her to have dinner with him Thursday evening because he had a poker game the following night with the guys, and it would run late. So, she'd agreed to dinner Thursday instead.

Alexis walked toward their table at The Warsaw in her classic work-look—a straight skirt, button-down silk blouse, and high heels. He couldn't wait to have every one of those items strewn across his bedroom floor.

As she came closer, he rose. The anxious expression on her face told him something was on her mind. He leaned down and kissed her cheek.

"Hello, gorgeous. You look like you could use a drink."

She exhaled and took the seat beside him. "That would be great."

The waitress approached. "Can I start you off with a drink, ma'am?"

Derek cut in, "If you'd like wine, I can order a bottle now, and we can finish it with dinner."

"That sounds great. Red or white, I don't care."

That was unusual. His girl was more decisive than that.

She always knew what she wanted—for anything, anytime.

He ordered a full-bodied chardonnay and an appetizer to share.

"Care to talk about it?"

She glanced his way, then reached for her water glass. He could tell that she debated disclosing personal topics of discussion. Hell, he'd known that for the past month they'd been dating. Not that she would call it dating. No, to Lexi, they were merely fuck buddies. They were together for one reason and one reason only. Revealing anything personal, even things about her business, was off-limits.

He mentally shook his head. It would take time to crack the heavily fortified shell she had carefully constructed around herself. Derek wondered who had wronged her, and how many people were allowed to see the real Lexi. He'd heard a bit about her good friend Rachel; she definitely got to see the real Lexi.

If he could be patient, he had to believe with time she'd soften to him too. "Okay. Wanna hear about my day?"

"If you want to tell me." That was his sassy girl, trying her very best to keep her distance.

"I had a decent week. Had a great meeting with a lender, got some good research analysis for potential future products, and our inventory sell-through rate looks steady. Reporting takes up the majority of my time, but so far, even with the tumultuous market lately, I think we stand to make our goals for the year."

Her eyes were pensive with an intensity he'd never seen before. Derek prided himself on learning all her facial expressions, but this one was new.

Is she concerned about her numbers?

"Sounds like you've been busy."

Derek shrugged. "Not as busy as you." He leaned in close and lowered his voice for her ears only. "I find lots of sex to be a healthy way to create balance in one's life." He winked though he was serious. Not only was he concerned about her working herself to the bone, but he also wanted to see her more often than just the weekends.

"So, you're prescribing more sex?" She grinned.

The appetizer arrived. They ordered their entrees, and he poured her more wine.

The dinner conversation continued, but Lexi revealed very little worth of substance. She visibly relaxed over her second glass of wine. Her shoulders loosened up, she swatted him once on the arm, and her smile returned.

Dinner was as excellent as he'd expected. They were nearly done with their meal when Lexi hesitated, but then said, "Something doesn't feel right."

Derek's heart turned over. He swallowed his bite and followed it with a gulp of wine. Was she concerned about their relationship? "How so?"

She'd been staring out the window into the night, the streetlights illuminating the road and sidewalk. "I got the numbers from my comptroller, and something doesn't feel right."

He exhaled in relief.

She met his gaze. "I'm pretty good at mentally keeping track of the numbers every week when they come in from the stores and online. So, every quarter and every year, I'm not surprised."

"Until now."

"Exactly."

"Have the books been audited?"

"Yes, though not by an outside auditor."

That wasn't necessary for a private company. Public companies hired outside auditors to verify the books, but Derek had done his research. When he'd learned about Lexi's company, he did a quick internet search and read up on it. She had a great little company, that was for sure, but it was private. Lexi had the majority share, with two other investors owning twenty-five percent.

He and Lexi sipped from their wineglasses. He had the solution, but he doubted she'd like it.

"Do you think the numbers are too high or too low?"

"Too low."

He nodded. *Here goes nothin'.* "I have an idea."

She glanced up from her plate.

"Give me your books and let me do a once-over. I might see something that was missed."

She furrowed her brow. "I couldn't ask you to do that."

"You're not. I'm offering."

Silence dragged.

"It's what I do for living, Lex. Trust your gut—if something feels off, there's likely a reason."

Her perfect lips scrunched up.

"Send me this year's, plus the last two just in case. I can look it over this weekend."

She sighed into her wineglass. "Okay. I'll send them in the morning. Now, can we get out of here? I haven't had an orgasm in five days."

He laughed and flagged down the waitress. "Sure."

Lexi didn't know how she felt about having Derek peruse her books. She was proud of her company but hated the idea of needing outside help. Being self-sufficient was Lexi's *modus operandi*.

Ultimately, she conceded because not knowing the answer was worse than having someone else look over her books.

They arrived at Derek's condo, and she walked toward the wall of windows. In another hour, the sunlight would be gone, and the view dark. She stared in awe at the water.

"Care for a glass of wine?"

She pivoted toward his voice in the kitchen. "Yes, please."

He joined her and handed her the wineglass, clinked them lightly together, and sipped.

"I have an observation."

The corner of his lip curved. "I bet you do."

"No personal items, no photos. Why?"

He glanced to the sofa. "Sit."

She took a seat next to him, resting her wine on the cocktail table.

"I guess I hadn't paid much attention, but I'm not very close to my parents and I have no brothers and sisters." He sipped from the glass and set it down next to hers.

Another parallel.

He lifted her leg she'd crossed over the other and eased her high heel from her foot. She'd give him this: he pampered the fuck out of her, and she loved it.

He continued the movement with the other foot, then swung them over his lap. "As I told you, my parents divorced when I was twelve. Dad is a womanizer to this day. He likes women he can manipulate or control."

Lexi bit back a moan when Derek dug into her arches. His story saddened her. Lexi wasn't close to her stepfather, but she still saw her mom and dad now and again. Neither parent was perfect, but there was still mutual admiration and respect between each other.

"Mom has low self-esteem. She's on husband number four. Dad is rich, so he got primary custody. He taught me all kinds of weird, lame stuff about women. 'Don't date the smart ones, they'll emasculate you and screw you over.'"

Nope, men can do the screwing over too, Lexi thought.

"'Women are okay to have a good time with, and when

you're bored, leave.' Which was exactly how he ran his life."

"What a dick statement."

"Agreed. I used to be close to my dad, but it changed my senior year in college."

That was the second time he'd specifically mentioned that time period in his life.

"What happened?" she asked.

Derek's hands massaged up her calves. "He hit on my girlfriend."

Her head jerked off the cushion. "What an asshole."

"Yup. So, I basically cut him out of my life. There's a trust fund that I haven't touched. From that point on, I did everything myself, paid for things with money I'd earned."

"You've done well, Derek, without him."

"Thank you."

They sat in silence, Derek massaging her feet and legs, her head resting against the arm of the sofa with her eyes closed.

His hands crept higher, and she didn't stop him. In the short month or so they'd been together, Lexi had quickly learned anytime she turned her body over to Derek, she was satisfied. More than satisfied.

He hiked her skirt higher and leaned down closer to kiss her thighs. His fingertips glossed over the lace trim of her panties and lingered there.

"You need to be naked," he whispered over her skin.

She opened her eyes to see his hand outstretched. She

grasped it and rose.

His lips instantly covered hers, his tongue gliding along hers. He began unfastening the buttons on her blouse as she ran her hands under his fine knit polo shirt. When he broke the kiss, he whipped off the shirt, and she dropped hers to the sofa.

He led her to the bedroom, then slipped off his shoes and loosened his pants. "Come here, gorgeous." His deep tone sent shivers over her body, residing deep into her core.

She approached him by the bed and let him devour her with his lips, his tongue, and his hands. He stripped her out of her skirt and reached for the clasp on her bra when she pushed against his chest.

The sun was slowly going down, but still... "Don't you have any drapes we can close?"

"Alexis, I'm on the twenty-eighth floor of a fifty-five-story building facing the bay. Who's gonna see us?"

He had a point—and she didn't see any window coverings. "Don't you at least have drapes for when you sleep?"

He shook his head. "Don't need them. I get up before the sun."

Wow! He didn't sleep much. Sleep was one of her favorite things to do.

He pulled her back against his bare-naked chest and flipped off her bra.

One of her favorite things.

Her panties soon followed, and he hoisted her onto his high bed. He'd probably had it specially made since he was so tall.

He wasted no time claiming her naked body, starting from the top and working his way south. Finally, he stopped to love on her breasts, teasing her nipples. She wished she had more than B-cup boobs, but Derek didn't seem to care.

Finally, his tongue caressed her eager clit, and she moaned long and low.

This man had a talented mouth. He was talented in quite a few ways if she really thought about it.

He swirled over her hot button and drove in two fingers.

"Unh." Her hands gripped his hair, and her hips lightly pulsed, meeting the amazing sensation his tongue gave her.

The twitch of her pussy muscles gripped Derek's fingers. He added a third finger and sent her over the ever-lovin' edge. Oh God, this was just what she needed. Fuck, if sex wasn't the cure for all her ails.

Derek stood, and she expected him to dive into her—but instead he walked to the other side of the bed, grabbed her arms at her pits, and dragged her to the edge.

Her heart skipped a beat at the sudden change in position, but then she saw what he had planned. Her head near the edge of the bed, and Derek opening his pants.

Yes. She'd never given head upside down, but she could do this.

She scooted another few inches to let her head fall over

the edge of the mattress and opened her mouth. She didn't even bother to reach for him.

"You look ready, my angel."

He slowly slid his cock into her open mouth, and her lips closed around him. He pushed and pulled, every stroke gaining another inch in her mouth. When he hit the back of her throat, she focused on staying open.

"Fuck, babygirl."

Lexi could see out of her periphery as Derek grabbed one of the posters of his bed for purchase.

He growled and continued to pulse his hips. His free hand roamed her torso and pussy for more playtime.

She reached up to hold him and stroked him as her mouth sucked. She gripped one hand at his ass cheek to bring him into her mouth more.

The gag reflex was incredibly low in this position. She briefly wondered if he'd learned that fact on another woman on this very bed. She pushed the thought from her mind. And just in time. Derek let out a groan as his ejaculate hit the back of her throat. She swallowed him down.

"Holy fuck," he panted out.

Chapter Ten

LEXI ROLLED OVER and felt something warm under her palm. The bed was particularly relaxing that morning. She didn't want to get up. She could stay asleep a while longer because her alarm would wake her.

The warmth grew under her hand, so she decided to assess where it was coming from.

Lexi opened her eyes to find Derek sound asleep on his back, her hand on his upper arm.

She could see everything which meant the sun was up. Blinking, she focused harder. They were in his bed. Okay, that's right. Dinner and then...

Oh, wait! Fuck! She'd fallen asleep at his place.

Crap! She never did that—well not since Dillion.

She sprung up in a panic. The clock on his side of the bed read seven-ten.

She took in a breath. It was not planned but not terrible. She didn't usually go into the office on the weekends.

Derek groaned and turned into her, his arm hooking

around her hips. "Morning, sexy."

His eyes were still closed. He had an adorable sleep-face.

"I thought you didn't sleep past sunrise."

"I don't," he grumbled.

"Yeah, well…" Lexi looked out his window, taking in the panoramic ocean in the distance. She would love a view like that one day, but not yet. Her company was still growing.

Her ears perked in the near silence. Was that her phone alarm? Of course, it was sitting in her purse on the floor. She should have turned it off for the weekend.

Oh, wait! It's Friday. Not Saturday or Sunday. She had work; she had an eight o'clock breakfast meeting with a new prospect.

"Fuck." She jumped from the bed and bent to pick up her clothes.

"What's wrong," Mr. Sleepy asked.

"It's Friday. I have a meeting. I didn't hear my alarm."

"What time is it?"

"Seven-ten." She ran to the living room and began to dress.

"Fuck."

"Exactly," she called back.

He strolled into the room buck naked, sporting some delicious wood, but that would have to wait. She was already running late. Damn! She never fell asleep at a man's place. Ever.

"I can't believe I slept that long." He stretched and groaned.

"Me either." In some semblance of togetherness, she slipped on her heels and grabbed her purse. "I'm outta here. Have fun playing poker tonight."

He grabbed her wrist, pulling her into his hard form, and pecked her lips. "Tomorrow. I'll pick you up for dinner."

"Okay, fine." She raced to the elevator, hoping a taxi would be close by when she made it to the ground floor.

She smoothed her hair in the elevator reflection. Double damn! Doing the walk of shame was not her thing. Oh well, there was nothing she could do about it now.

Derek walked into the kitchen to start a pot of coffee.

Wow. Just wow.

He'd slept eight hours. When was the last time he'd done that? College?

And it sounded like Lexi'd had a great sleep too. Probably after a stressful day, she needed it.

God, it felt good, having her in his bed. He'd woken her one time, probably around midnight, to make love to her. She'd gotten so wet, he slid into her warm heat like she was made for him. She'd gripped the headboard in her orgasm, and he'd taken advantage of the leverage and pounded into her. He feared he'd taken it too far, but she'd only moaned at his animalistic thrusts.

It was really quite simple. She was perfect for him, and

he for her. Now, to convince her. Achieving world peace might be easier.

With a mug of hot black coffee, he strode to his bathroom and turned the shower on full blast.

"That was the first time I've slept more than six hours in years," he told his reflection and smirked. He had every reason to thank Lexi for it.

Strolling into work at ten o'clock rarely happened to Derek. He'd planned his workweeks to be up early, hit the gym, shower, grab breakfast, and beat the rush-hour traffic to the office. That was the cost he paid for living in Baybrook. He'd have to drive thirty-five minutes without traffic to make it in to Vigers at a reasonable time.

With traffic? Forget about it.

He'd phoned his admin that morning from the car. Marta was a sixty-year-old, completely gray-haired firecracker of an assistant. She ran a tight ship. She'd kept her surprise to a minimum when he'd called, and said she'd adjust his meetings accordingly.

But really, nothing could spoil his great mood. He and Lexi had a connection that was unquestionable.

Renee had told him love would be like this.

Renee Belcher had been his boss at a high-volume, family-style restaurant during his senior year of college. After he'd told his dad he didn't need his money and he would finish school on his own, he'd taken the job to help pay for tuition. He'd scrimped and saved, got a student loan, and worked as much as he could handle to make sure he graduated.

Renee was a sharp businesswoman. He'd learned a ton from her, but he'd also learned about love. She'd put it together real fast that Derek kept his distance from relationships. She'd said, *You're a good-looking guy. Why don't you have a girlfriend?*

Eventually, he ended up telling her the entire story with his father. Renee's statement had been similar to Lexi's: *Dickhead.*

Renee had taken on a motherly role and somehow felt it her responsibility to teach—really, reteach—Derek about love, in addition to business. She'd taught him about the "emotional bank account." *Derek, you can make deposits, or you can make withdrawals. Making deposits is better. Deposits help soothe emotions for when you accidentally make a withdrawal.*

Renee had taught him a woman who responded "fine" was probably the furthest thing from fine. She'd introduced him to *The 5 Love Languages.* And *Derek, help her get what she wants, and she'll help you get what you want.*

The education had been invaluable.

Derek took all those lessons to heart. Renee had been happily married over twenty years at that point so that had counted for something in his eyes.

Derek had realized after graduation that he was

attracted to strong women. Women who didn't "need" him but wanted him. Women with self-confidence and a willingness to succeed.

Alexis had all that in spades.

He was softening her but had yet to crack her shell. He didn't know how deep her wounds were, but he was a patient man. *Slow and steady wins the race.*

Booting up his computer, Derek had ten minutes before his next meeting—his first meeting of the day—and he already felt like his day was half over.

He could chuckle at himself. He was a work-early and stay-late kinda guy. Starting his day late was foreign to him.

And all over a woman.

Speaking of the woman, Lexi's email was at the top of his inbox. He saw the attached financials from the past three years. Good. He'd dive into that his first free minute.

Her note was the straight-forward, Lexi-style: *Thanks*.

His comptroller, Earl, wrapped on his door, breaking the runaway thoughts of the sexy woman in his bed that morning. Earl was an accountant from way back. His gray hair and slight hunch gave away his years, but he was a crackerjack with numbers. He had more knowledge about accounting and financial law than just about anybody on the planet.

Vigers' year financially had been a bit of a rollercoaster. Supply-chain issues Quarter One had affected sales, and Wall Street was not happy. Now Earl sat across from him with a file folder, ready to review the first-half of the year's events.

He hadn't lied to Lexi, or anyone else, about making their yearly sales goals, but it was turning out to be an uphill battle.

"Derek, here are the numbers I have for the first half of the year." Earl handed him a print-out. "We officially made the bad debt write-off for Kompak's bankruptcy."

"Okay." Derek scanned the report, thankfully seeing more black than red. "There's the one-time write-off from the manufacturing machinery."

"Yeah, boss. And with the capital allocation for the new equipment, that looks to be a hit of three percent to net profit."

Ouch. Well, they had two identical manufacturing facilities, so every expense was times two. "Obsolescence is unavoidable, Earl."

The man nodded and talked through several more figures and highlights.

"And are these the latest sales forecasts?"

They discussed the projections—new products, retiring products, and the expected effect on the income statement.

"The only other thing we need to be aware of is the growing concern for data security. It's certainly being talked about more in the press, and of course, our customers are looking for new ways to protect themselves." Earl closed his folder and sighed.

Having had several conversations over the past three

years with Fredrick, their head of R&D, he was very aware of the data security issue. He knew the Fortune 500 were especially targeted for attacks. If Vigers' customers were concerned about it, then so was everyone in the company, including the bean counters. He made a mental note to get on Fredrick's calendar soon for an update.

He gazed at his valued employee, someday soon to be a retiree. "We have to look at this as an opportunity, not a threat, Earl."

~

Lexi was thinking about Derek more and more—day or night, even at work. They were also spending a lot of time together during the weekends. It had been over a week now that Derek had her financials in the hopes of finding a discrepancy.

She wasn't sure any of this was a good idea.

Saturday morning, she rolled over to an empty bed. She'd pushed Derek out the door around one in the morning. She wanted it this way, at least she thought she did. Maybe an occasional sleepover wouldn't be a bad idea...

See! She yelled at herself. Derek was becoming ingrained into her being, her soul, her life! This was not supposed to happen. This thing between them was just supposed to be sex.

Maybe she should plan a trip to Florida to see her old college roommate and give her and Derek some space. *Not with the Forest Ridge location just opening.* She sighed.

Her phone buzzed with a text. Speak of the devil.

Be ready at 4. I have an errand to run and need your help. Dinner and dessert back at my place.

A prime example of spending more time together. She nibbled on her lip; she should say no. She typed her reply.

Fine. I'll be waiting.

What exactly did he need to do that involved her joining him? A little thrill raced through her—which she patently ignored—as she hopped out of bed.

The day flew by, and promptly at four Derek was outside her apartment building.

Lexi folded herself into the front seat of his sedan, and before she could buckle up, he gripped the back of her neck and drew her close for a tongue kiss. There was no tentativeness or gentleness. It was like he wanted to own her.

"Well, hello."

He grinned. "Ready?"

"Sure. Where are we going?"

"To a nursery."

What? Lexi let out a shaky exhale, willing herself to remain composed. *What is he talking about?*

"A nursery for plants, not the other kind," he said with

mischief in his eyes.

"Asshole," she said under her breath but loud enough for him to hear.

He chuckled. "I want some plants at my place. I thought you could help me pick out a few."

"I don't know much about flora or fauna."

He shrugged like it didn't make a bit of difference.

They meandered through the plant shop for almost an hour, discussing which variety to put where in his condo. Tall ones, short ones, and various pots to go along with the selection. He favored sages and deep blues with orange accents.

"I want to warm up the place a bit, so I'm making some changes. You said I had nothing personal there," he said at one point.

She thought his place was perfect. It was a frickin' oasis in the sky. The only thing she'd like would be for him to live closer to her so they wouldn't spend so much time in traffic.

Ugh! Scratch that!

"Okay, that should do it." Derek pushed the cart to the checkout, and thirty minutes after that, they were pulling into his parking garage.

They carried the plants into his condo and set them up by the expansive windows.

He rested his hands on his hips and stepped back. "I like it. Let's take these three into the bedroom."

She carried one plant as she followed him into his

bedroom. She noticed the change immediately. "You got another nightstand."

He twisted slightly and looked at her. "I did. So you can use it."

Was that his way of saying it was for her? *Oh no. No, no, no.*

He must have read her apprehension because he crossed the floor in four steps and stood before her. He was confident as he said, "Lexi, I want you to have this to use when you sleep over. A place for your cell phone so you're never late. I even have a notepad in case you get an idea in the middle of the night."

Wow. Did he really do that?

He took the plant out of her hands and set it by the other two.

She brushed her palms together. "So, you want me to sleep over?"

"Yes. This happens occasionally when people date."

She swallowed hard. *Date?* "We're having sex."

"Don't overthink this." He cupped her jaw, then kissed her and hovered over her lips. "When you sleep here it's easy for me to fuck you whenever I want. Not to mention, *I* sleep better."

She rocked her head back. "You do?"

"Yes. Now, take a look around. You're sleeping here tonight. I'm going to have dinner brought up." His tone was matter-of-fact. No expectations, just, a nightstand.

He strode from the room.

Okay, there were so many things in that statement she could hardly process all of it.

Look around.

Well, she'd already seen the nightstand, so she opened the closet door.

Shit! Hanging on the right side, close to the door, were three straight skirts and four button-down designer blouses. Her hand stroked down the material. She moved to the dresser. The second drawer she opened held a small bundle of panties and bras, all in her size, with the tags still on them.

She felt lightheaded.

He wanted her to sleep over.

God, did she want that? Could she do that?

She strode to the bathroom, and in a basket on the vanity were her favorite skin care items and a few cosmetics plus a packaged toothbrush.

Oh God, this was too much. Did he expect her to move in? This was *way* too much.

He'd paid attention to her preferences when he spent time at her place and replicated it here.

She could hear Rachel's voice in her head: *Lex, that is so sweet. He cares about you.*

And it was sweet, but that didn't change that Lexi felt torn. The clothes, the makeup, the matching nightstand—how was she supposed to handle this?

Derek said, "Hey," from the doorway.

Lexi spun around.

Chapter Eleven

DEREK COULD SEE how difficult this was for Lexi and prayed he hadn't gone too far. Her face was pale, and her shoulders were stiff. But really, they'd been exclusive for almost two months now. They were mature adults, dating only each other, and there was nothing wrong with her having a few things at his place. And he sure as shit knew she wouldn't willingly bring anything over, so he'd taken it upon himself to make it happen.

He handed her the glass of chardonnay he'd just poured. "I know that isn't everything," he nudged his chin toward the basket, "so feel free to bring anything else you want."

She downed nearly half the wine, and he held back a chuckle.

"This...um...this is too much."

He stepped closer and clasped her chin. "It's not. Don't overthink it, Lex. You spend time here so why not make it a little more hassle-free." He kissed her lips for several long moments before he pulled back.

"If dinner wasn't almost here, I'd lean you over this counter and fuck you from behind." He pecked her lips once more. "C'mon."

She took the hand he offered and followed him into the main living area. He'd set the table and lit several candles. The doorbell rang. *Right on time.*

Derek wasn't much of a cook. He could do some basic stuff; being a bachelor, you had to know how to prepare at least a few things. Another necessity was learning the best places to eat. Baybrook had a five-star restaurant just one block from his condo building. They normally didn't do delivery, but he'd tipped them well on the occasion he'd entertained a lady and wanted to impress. None of that mattered now.

Lexi was the only woman that he cared about impressing.

He'd never allowed a lady to keep things at his place, not really. Not until now. He thought about disclosing that to Lexi but feared it might freak her out more.

He opened the door, handled the overstuffed bags of food, and gave the delivery boy a generous tip.

He strode to his dining table and lifted containers from the bag. "I wasn't sure what you'd be hungry for, so we have a few selections to choose from."

Derek glanced up as she stood beside him, holding an almost empty wineglass.

He motioned for her to sit as he set out scallops, beef

medallions, chicken piccata, and bacon-wrapped filet, plus an assortment of sides. Whatever they didn't eat would make for great leftovers during the week.

The dinner started off quiet, but as Lexi ate the color returned to her face. "Thank you for...everything." She motioned her hand, barely lifting it from the table, toward the bedroom.

He knew that took effort. "You're welcome."

Slowly, she relaxed and could talk more about her week. Derek told her he'd begun reviewing her financials but hadn't found anything yet. Shopping for Lexi had taken precedence and having things delivered certainly helped.

After dinner, they cleared the table and brought their wineglasses to the sofa. They sat, but she quickly stood and stared out the window, now dark outside.

Tension rose in his shoulders wondering what was on her mind.

Is she thinking about the sleepover tonight?

"Are you free next Saturday?"

He nearly swallowed his tongue. Those were words he never thought would come out of Lexi's mouth. "Yes, I believe I am." Since meeting Lexi, he'd done everything in his power to clear his calendar for the weekends. For her.

She turned to face him. "We've been invited to my friend's house for dinner with her fiancé."

"That sounds great. I'd love to go." Derek wondered if this was the couple who'd had an engagement party months ago at Bogart's...the first time he'd laid eyes on Lexi. For an opportunity to meet her friends, people important to her, he'd jump on it.

Lexi stayed in place, still staring out at the dark. When she didn't say anything else, he stood and crossed to her side. He caressed a hand up her arm. "I know this is a lot to process. Let's think about something else for a couple hours, all right?"

He took the glass out of her hand and set it on an end table. He brushed a finger over her jaw and leaned down to peck her lips, licking at the seam and running his tongue against her teeth.

Sliding his hand over her throat, he gently closed it around her delicate neck. The pressure was so light she could knock him away in a flash, but it was possessive. She knew it. He knew it. And she let him.

He'd constantly keep her guessing, keep her curious, wondering what he would do next. Lexi needed that, and so did he, which was why they were such a perfect couple.

As he feasted on her mouth with a hand at her throat, he freed her of her clothes—first the blouse, then the skirt, and lastly her lingerie.

She stood before him in only her shoes.

He broke the kiss, and still holding her throat, stepped back to admire her form.

"Perfect. So fucking perfect. Now lay down on my sofa. Keep the heels on."

Her cheeks were already flushed, and her breathing sped. She lay on her back—one foot on the floor, and the other leg draped across the back of the couch.

Fuck me!

She was offering herself to him. Her pussy glistened, and he couldn't wait to dive in.

He undressed lazily, taking his time, and laid his clothes at the far end of the sofa. "Lexi, you look so good, I could take a picture."

Her eyes glimmered, but she didn't otherwise budge or say a word.

"Arms overhead."

She reached her arms up and gripped the edge of the couch—her head cradled in a pillow. Spread out like that, she looked like a fucking centerfold. Gorgeous, plump lips waited for him to devour.

He took himself in hand and pumped a few times, alleviating some of the pressure.

She watched him; her blue eyes dark as midnight.

He leaned down and blew against her sex.

She writhed and he did it again, giving her an inkling of what he had planned.

Tonight, he would torture her with extreme pleasure. He would take his time, dragging out the ecstasy, until she came all over him with the best orgasm of her entire life.

He swiped the tip of his tongue through her slit and to her tiny bundle.

She squirmed again and mewled.

He played with her a few more times and stopped.

Her eyes opened, and he rose. "Don't move," he commanded. He strode to his nightstand and retrieved a new vibrator he'd also purchased for her this past week.

Her gaze tracked him as he returned to the sofa. She was just as he'd left her.

Kneeling down, he swiped her pussy and clit several more times, her clit larger than ever now. He poised the vibe at her entrance and slowly pushed it through the slickness.

"I want your dick, not that piece of plastic."

"*Tsk, tsk.* Anytime, anywhere. I pick."

He pushed the device in farther and her pussy sucked it in. He slowly stroked in and out of her.

A light sheen of sweat gathered over her brow. She was close to exploding.

He licked her more, but even softer than before. That was the only place they connected—a hair's width between his tongue and her sweet honeypot.

Her writhing stilled as she realized she might lose their precious connection. Even as her hips lifted off the sofa, he'd back up.

She was sexy as fuck, and it was all he could do not to ram into her right then.

She panted and groaned out her frustration at not getting the delicious pressure she needed to orgasm.

His strokes with the vibe slowed even more, and his

tongue hadn't stopped its teasing.

Her hips had to be eight inches off the sofa. She sought her pleasure, craved her pleasure. Since he was the one to give it to her, she would come to seek him, crave him, want him more than just about anything else in her world.

All Derek had ever tackled, accomplished, learned, tried, and even the failed lessons, had led to this moment. Everything was preparation for this woman, this perfect woman, to enter his life. He knew how to treat her, care for her, love her, and how to fuck her. She would need no other man.

He pulled back. "Don't move." He loved commanding her, mostly because he knew she was coming to trust him. Trust that he wouldn't hurt her in any way.

He slid out the vibe and set it on the floor, then he knelt on the sofa, between her spread, raised hips. He made her hold her position for him as he dragged his cock through her wet slit and over her burgeoning clit.

"Derek," she pleaded.

He toyed with her delicious pussy some more, smearing his pre-cum over her like he was an animal marking his territory. Again, only one simple connection point, but they didn't need more. She didn't need more. She knew he held all her pleasure and regardless of how much skin-to-skin contact there might be, she was his. They belonged to each other, and one day she would know that fact.

He gingerly pushed through her swollen, wet pussy.

They both groaned at finally being able to savor the contact. He pulled back and thrust inside, pushing against her channel walls.

She writhed, her body begging for release.

He gripped her hips, and her eyes flew open. Now, they would have their release.

Firmly holding her hips, he dragged her onto his cock. He rocked her back and forward as he took in the perfect image of her accepting him deep into her.

Her tiny screeches increased, and her breasts jostled.

He tugged on her hips again, hitting her sweet spot deep inside.

Finally, she screamed out his name as she thrashed before him.

His grip tightened. He wouldn't let her go. His seed burst free, and with a growl, he held her flush as his cock jerked and twitched inside her gripping channel.

He collapsed after several beats, gasping into her neck. When her arms and legs snaked around him, he knew he was one step closer to having her in his bed and in his life permanently.

Chapter Twelve

THE PAST WEEK had been an emotional whirlwind since Derek had bought her a toothbrush for his place. Lexi had been torn between fuck buddies and more. She knew her emotions were very much at risk, and yet she couldn't stop being with Derek or thinking about him. She looked forward to seeing and hearing from him.

He'd bought her clothes and a nightstand *and* wanted her to sleep over!

It had been a rollercoaster since last weekend. When she thought about it too hard, her stomach twisted into knots. Then she would talk to him or see him, and the tension vanished.

Having him meet Rachel and Hunter was something she hadn't done with her other "friends" so this was different but she would go along with it because she trusted him.

Derek parked in front of Rachel's house and gave her hand a little squeeze before stepping out.

Lexi was nervous, and she knew she needn't be. Rachel

and Hunter were a terrific couple and wonderful people individually. Her BFF had picked a winner of a fiancé.

The door swung open, and Rachel's exuberant smile hit Lexi to her core. Rachel had been the orchestrator—or instigator—of this evening. Lexi had been reluctant, but now seeing her friend's smile, she was glad she'd agreed.

"Come in." Rachel embraced her like they hadn't just seen each other the prior week—then she raised up to hug Derek. "Hi!"

"Rachel, this is Derek Hollister. Derek, this is Rachel Johnson." Hunter approached. "And this is her fiancé, Hunter Baron." Derek was about two inches taller than Hunter with darker hair. The muscles on both men showed everyone they knew how to take care of themselves.

Derek offered smiles and a hand to Hunter. "Great to meet you both."

"Let's have a drink before dinner." Everyone followed Rachel into the kitchen where something incredible scented the air. Savory with a hint of sweetness.

"Rach, what are you cooking?"

Rachel slipped off the apron she wore over her summer dress. "Chicken marsala."

"Smells great," Lexi said as she opened the lid to the electric frying pan.

"Sure does." Derek accepted a beer from Hunter.

"So, Derek, Lexi tells us you work for Vigers. How do you like it?" Hunter popped the top off his beer bottle and took a swig.

"I like it. I've been there eight years now."

"Good company. What do you do?" Hunter leaned back against the counter.

Derek raised his beer toward Lexi. "I'm the head bean counter."

Everyone laughed.

Lexi knew he was being modest and guessed that was probably *not* the first time he'd used that line.

"Have y'all set a date yet?" Derek asked.

Hunter looped an arm around Rachel's waist and kissed the top of her head. "As soon as I can get her on a plane to Vegas."

Derek chuckled and Rachel swatted Hunter on the stomach. "We're looking at the fall. Just trying to narrow down the venue."

Lexi briefly wondered if she would invite Derek to be her Plus One. Would they still be, whatever they were, in four months? She'd never miss her bestie's wedding, but she might just go alone. Not thinking too far ahead when it came to men was Lexi's preference. It reduced the chances of being disappointed and let down.

"Lex, help me set the dining room table, would ya?" Rachel placed a stack of plates on the island in front of Lexi, then turned to the silverware drawer.

Lexi lifted the plates and followed Rachel, who already had her fine tablecloth and napkins in place with several votive candles lit.

Rachel leaned in close. "He's cute, Lex. And nice." She grinned.

Of course, Derek *seemed* nice. He didn't get to the position he was in at work without knowing how to play a part. "So far."

Rachel tipped her head and narrowed her eyes. "Lexi, give this one a chance, would you? You deserve to be happy."

Lexi lifted a brow. A. She was happy. And B. Rachel knew Lexi didn't do the long-term relationship thing anymore. That shipped had sailed.

"You know what I mean. Derek could be the real deal. Not all men are jerks."

She didn't want to burst her friend's bubble. Being skeptical of the male species was in Lexi's nature, but she nodded and agreed for Rachel's sake.

What if Lexi didn't *need* happily ever after like Rachel? And she didn't want to be pushed. And what if her life was just fine in the "single" lane?

Derek cut into his chicken and took a bite. *Mmm.*

He'd recognized Rachel and Hunter immediately from the night of their engagement party at Bogart's. The glow of being in love was easy to spot.

That was the same night he'd first seen Lexi. He'd known right away that he had to meet her and learn everything about her. His patience had paid off. Here he was, sitting at the dinner table with the most important person in Lexi's life, chatting and laughing, just as friends would.

Derek, attuned to Lexi, realized that she was nervous about their intimate dinner at Rachel's. He'd bet his last Benjamin that he was the first dinner date she'd brought to her friend's place in a long time.

He conversed easily with Hunter, who seemed like a helluva guy and obviously cared a lot for Rachel. The gleam in his eye gave away how much Hunter loved Rachel.

Hunter told him about his company and a few interesting stories of his clients. There was also some discussion about Rachel's two children from a previous marriage.

"Maybe the next time y'all come over, I'll have the kids here and we'll barbeque out back." Rachel looped a lock of hair behind her ear.

Rachel had made a good life for herself. Derek could already see she was a wonderful cook, had a great fiancé, and likely had equally super kids. Meeting her kids, getting to know them both more, would be the highlight of his week.

Lexi's back straightened imperceptibly, but he saw it.

Discussion of the future made her squirm. His girl didn't like to commit to anything. Last Saturday, when he'd given her a little setup at his place, probably had her searching for a reason to run. Distracting her with orgasms helped "soften the blow." Sunday night, he hadn't batted an eye when she'd wanted to sleep at her own place.

He could almost chuckle out loud at the plans he had for her and for them together. "That would be great. The view of that lake is amazing. So peaceful."

"It is." Rachel smiled before sipping her chardonnay.

After several minutes of finishing off the chicken and mushrooms, Derek leaned back in his chair. "Rachel, that was incredible. Thank you."

"It was, babe." Hunter winked at her from across the rectangular table.

"Derek, why don't you help me with the dessert and coffee?"

"You got it." He didn't need to be told twice.

He followed Rachel into the kitchen, and she quickly pulled him farther away from the dining room entryway. "Derek, you might've noticed Lexi has a few walls built around her. Frankly, she has good reason. But please don't give up on her. Lately, she's been happier and a lot less stressed, even as she's down one designer. I'm pretty sure it has to do with you." Rachel squeezed his hand.

"Thanks for that."

"I love my friend like a sister. She deserves to be happy. And I have a good feeling about you. I think you want the best for her too."

He nodded.

"So, all I'm asking is for you to be patient with her. I gotta believe she'll come around."

That was absolute music to his ears. Of course, he

wouldn't give up on Lexi, but it was good to hear her best friend was on his side. "Absolutely."

Chapter Thirteen

TUESDAY AFTER LUNCH, Derek called Lexi at her office.

"Hello?" She sounded surprised to hear from him, probably because he hadn't called her cell phone as he normally did.

"Lexi. I think I found your accounting error. Come over tonight so we can talk about it." He wished it hadn't taken so long, but with work and prepping his place for Lexi, he just didn't have the extra time he thought he would.

"Oh shit. That bad, huh?" She sighed over the phone.

"We'll talk about it tonight." He disconnected the line before she could ask anything more.

Okay. Derek might be taking a few liberties with Lexi. For one, he'd found the error Sunday, but wanted an excuse to see her during the week. This weekend-only crap was getting old. Also, he wanted her to come to *his* place so he could convince her to sleep over.

He couldn't explain it, but he slept better with warm

Lexi in his bed. Even if he'd woken her in the middle of the night to do wonderfully nasty things to her body, he still felt incredibly rested in the morning.

She seemed rested too, not that she'd slept over often, even though she now had clothes at his place, but he was bound and determined to change that. Starting tonight.

Derek's office phone rang, pulling him from his daze.

"Fredrick, how's it going?"

"Good, busy." Fredrick's German accent had gotten easier for Derek to understand over the years. He had a key role at Vigers, and as the head of Research and Development for a major infrastructure tech company, there was never a dull moment.

"I know I've been hard to get a hold of lately. Sorry." Fredrick sighed.

Derek had tried to reach out a few times to discuss Vigers' future plans for additional security offerings. "I understand."

"I want a meeting with Jamie and all the lieutenants."

Jamie Almond was Vigers' CEO. "Sounds good. We're overdue. Want me to put it together?"

"Would you? That would be great."

"You bet. I'll send you a request once the time is set."

Data security was quickly and repeatedly becoming front-page news. With some incredible design and serious financial investment, Vigers was poised to capitalize on this urgent need. Derek would do his part to make sure Fredrick had his bankroll.

~

Lexi walked through the lobby of Derek's magnificent condo building.

"Evening, Ms. King," the guard called.

There were probably three or four guards, and Lexi had learned the names of all of them. She didn't know how long this "relationship" with Derek would continue, but for now it was going well…she wouldn't rock the boat. It would be nice to know a few people in Derek's life.

"Hi, Bill." She waved and pressed the button to head up to Derek's place.

She was excited that Derek had found the error, but also scared pea-green that it was something awful, and possibly worse than she'd originally feared. Her gut had told her the sales figures weren't accurate, but what if there was something on the expense side that was missed.

She rang the bell and was swiftly pulled inside, into Derek's arms, with his lips capturing hers in a kiss.

"Well, hello," she managed to get out when he released her.

"Hi, yourself. Come in." He pushed the door closed and strode to the kitchen.

Lexi placed her bag on the sideboard and walked into the kitchen where he stirred a pot on the stove. Remnants of ingredients rested on the counter and a cutting board. *Derek is cooking.* "Um, you're tonight's chef? I didn't think you were allowed in the kitchen if it wasn't for beer, water, or coffee."

"Ha. Ha," he replied, but with a twinkle in his eye. "I felt inspired."

She leaned against his side to peer into the pot. "It looks and smells like spaghetti sauce."

He smiled. "It is. I hope it tastes like it too."

She flipped her hair behind her shoulder. "If not, I'm sure one of your restaurants on speed-dial will happily bring up dinner."

He stuck out his tongue at her and covered the dish.

She couldn't help but laugh.

"This can sit for a bit. Here's what I found." Derek pointed to a folder on the counter. "Take a look and I'll pour us some wine."

She went to the other side of the peninsula and opened the manila folder. He'd printed out a few pages from her financials. A few things were circled. She studied the document and noticed sales figures were circled in red.

He came to her side and set down her wineglass. "It was a simple error, Lexi."

She braced herself for bad news. "Okay, so help me understand what I'm seeing."

He pointed to the sales figures from her River Oaks location. "One month of sales for this store was wrongly recorded as the figure from the same month last fiscal year." He then pointed to last year's figures. November had the same figure recorded for both years, when in fact this past November's sales had been higher.

"Something slipped through the cracks when the books were audited. It's not a big deal."

She glanced up at him to make sure he was serious. "Not a big deal?" These numbers hadn't been shared with her investors yet, but who's to say they wouldn't have missed the "hiccup" in sales?

"Not really. Whoever did the books just overlooked this wrong entry. It may help if going forward you have a second set of eyes on it for auditing."

That made sense. Gregory had audited these. It was unlike him to miss stuff. If necessary, she should think about getting someone else in that department who was qualified or just hire an outside firm.

"There's just one more thing, Lex." He peeled away the top page and pointed to another page he'd printed out. Some salaries were highlighted. "You utilize contract labor, right?"

She nodded.

"Well, they've been recorded as employees."

Her eyebrows pulled together as she studied the sheet. He was right. She would need to ask her team about this.

"There's a difference between an employee and a contractor—a difference that you'll need to account for."

Good God. Her books were a hot mess.

Lexi's face exuded concern. She probably had a

stressed-out, overworked employee who needed a nice long vacation before returning to his or her job. "It's a rather common error. Try not to worry about it."

"It is?"

"Yes. I promise. And as much as we use computers to do the number-crunching, it's still dependent on accurate information that a person needs to input."

She sipped a healthy gulp from her wineglass.

"Errors can still happen—in small, medium, or large companies."

"Okay."

"Whoever had been working on this likely needs a vacation."

She tipped her head to the side. "He works his ass off for me. He's got a soft spot in his heart for me and my company." She glanced back down at her paperwork.

Derek was still stuck on the "he" part. Of course, she had male employees. He just hadn't been prepared to hear of someone with such...affection for Lexi.

He didn't want to appear possessive, so he returned to the stove to check on the boiling pasta. Finally, he drained the water and began plating the food.

"Thanks so much for doing this." She walked up to him, stood on her tiptoes, and kissed his mouth.

Derek loved her show of affection. He wrapped his arms around her and kissed her back. "You're welcome. Glad I could help. You can make it up to me later." He winked and returned to his dinner prep.

It was a basic meal of spaghetti with meat sauce, a salad, and red wine. He thought it turned out decent, considering that was the first time he'd made it.

"Mmm. It's good, Derek," Lexi said in between bites.

And that was all the validation he needed.

After dinner, he did a light clean-up, refilled their wineglasses, and then joined her on the sofa. He took off her shoes and set her feet on his lap. "Lay back. Get comfortable."

She hesitated, but then reclined, resting her head against the arm of the sofa.

He massaged her feet as she closed her eyes and hummed her approval. He worked one foot at a time for several minutes, then graduated to her calves. When he ventured past her knees, he pushed her skirt higher, and blue panties peeked out.

Her breathing increased, but she didn't move a muscle, not even to open her eyes. She'd let Derek do what he wanted, and the fact that her trust in him was growing—that she'd allowed herself to trust him—made Derek want to jump for joy.

He knew it was trust of her body and not her heart, but it was still progress.

Suddenly, Lexi rose and stood before him. She made fast work of her blouse and skirt, leaving them in a puddle on the floor.

Good girl. You won't be wearing them again anyway to leave here.

She knelt before him and parted his legs. What would she do?

She opened his pants and freed his dick. When her lips came down on him, he nearly blew his load. He'd had a semi since the moment she'd walked through his door. Her mouth was warm and wet, coating him as she sucked him up and down. He slouched further on the sofa and relished the beauty of her exquisite mouth on him.

Then she stopped.

He opened his eyes as she straddled his lap and hovered over his crotch.

She tugged her panties aside, aligned his dick, and sank down.

"Fuck me," he breathed out as he gripped her hips, letting her ride him to her heart's content.

"I love how your body takes me in." He specifically used the L-word more often in their games; she needed to get used to hearing it.

"You're big."

"And yet you make room for me." There were multiple meanings in that statement, but Derek wouldn't give her time to think about it. He peeled down her bra straps, exposing her scrumptious nipples for him to feast.

He laved and sucked, occasionally feeling a tug on his cock from her pussy muscles. He loved finding all the spots on her body to excite her, all the ways to bring her pleasure.

He had ideas, so many fucking brilliant ideas. Slowly, he would play out each and every one—whether it was fucking on a balcony in broad daylight or going to a sex club—to give Lexi what she craved. Not just hot sex, but adventure, eroticism, escapism. In many ways, tearing her away from her life, forcing her to think about nothing and only feel, made her more grounded in her everyday life. Making a firm decision on a new designer, realizing she can't do it all, was a perfect case in point. He knew the old Lexi would have rationalized the additional workload on herself. Also, she was making room in her world for him. He was carving out space to the point where she would feel empty if she let him go.

If she let him go, he would feel empty. No doubt about it.

He reached down to circle a thumb over her clit.

She moaned but continued rocking over him.

He gripped the back of her neck, fastening her lips to his. He dove into her depths, fucking her mouth with his tongue like he fucked her pussy. She was glorious.

Lexi was so close she panted like a racehorse.

He captured her nipple again, sucking hard only to hear her cry out and grip his dick inside her. God, he loved it. How his body was made to please her, and hers to please him. He shot his load deep inside as they came together, moaning and moving wildly as one.

She collapsed over him, panting into his shoulder.

"You are fucking incredible," he whispered. "You're staying the night. I want to do that again, without clothes on."

"I knew you were going to say that."

He chuckled. "You owe me." Not really, because he would do anything for Lexi without a single thought to payback.

"I knew you were going to say that too."

He kissed the side of her head and smiled. This was his future wife. Given enough time, she would say, *I knew I was going to marry you.*

Chapter Fourteen

DEREK WALKED INTO the lab for the team meeting Fredrick had called. The space held gadgets, wiring, and raw materials; some areas were divided by glass partitions. This was the heart of Vigers, and Derek knew for a fact the room had been insulated in a way to prevent any electronic eavesdropping.

As Fredrick had asked, Derek set up the meeting to be in the lab so that everyone could see firsthand the technology and get an update on new products, specifically those centered on data security.

He was no dummy and realized Fredrick was getting ready for a big ask. Probably money for more equipment and personnel.

Vigers' CMO and their head of Production were already standing around chatting, and Jamie Almond, their CEO, followed behind Derek into the lab.

"Thanks for making it. Please gather around." Fredrick led everyone to a worktable. "Attackers are always trying to find and exploit vulnerabilities. These vulnerabilities can exist in a broad number of areas, including devices, data, applications, users, and locations.

"We've made some enhancements to our offerings for internet, intranet, and cloud-based computing. As Firewall and VPN technology improves so will Vigers' hardware, to keep up with the load demand and data throughput."

Derek lifted a router off the table to inspect.

"We need to enhance network performance," Fredrick held out his right palm, "and balance that with securing data shared between our customers' employees and data sources." He held out his left hand.

A glance at the men beside him told Derek they had a definite idea of what Fredrick was referring to.

"We've made some enhancements to our authenticators and dongles." Fredrick lifted a basic gadget to show. "In addition, we are seeing some excellent data come back on our new smartcard chip. Always a favorite of our customers."

Vigers had gained some incredibly impressive clients over the years, Fortune 1000 corporations mostly, but had some profitable accounts in the small- and mid-sized space as well.

The men nodded.

"On the high end, our hardware security module has been enhanced by the team. This offers outstanding physical protection and a range of service levels."

"High-end hardware with a high-end price tag," his

CMO, Darius, commented.

The men held up the various components. Derek knew the future of Vigers hinged on getting this right. The challenges of the nineties and early two-thousands of speed throughput, bandwidth, and internet connectivity all paled in comparison to what Vigers had to bring to the table now. If they didn't, some other company would, and they'd lose customers.

Derek tried to set up the conversation for the group to further recognize what was at stake. "Fredrick, I know we play a part in data security, but isn't it mostly a software issue?"

Fredrick shook his head repeatedly. "Cyberattacks are at an all-time high. The data doesn't lie. No one is safe—any company, no matter how big or small, can be at risk. It takes a multi-prong approach—hardware, software, users—to make data secure."

"Fredrick, it sounds like we're positioned to have a fairly extensive offering for our customers, yes?" Jamie asked.

Fredrick nodded but then leaned forward, resting his hands on the table. "*Ja.* It will take investment on our part, over the next few years. The good news is this concern, this solution, has value to our customers, and they'll pay for it."

He pulled a folder from a desk behind him and opened it, sliding it across the table. Derek read it—the estimates of what Fredrick needed over the next five years were steep. Then Derek glanced at the projected sales.

Whoa!

He looked up and Jamie's eyes were wide.

"Impressive," Darius chimed in.

"Agreed." Jamie glanced at Derek. "Would you and Fredrick be able to get together sometime and validate these numbers? I'd like to meet about this again in a few weeks. Perhaps in the conference room with some regional sales managers." He glanced around the table.

"Sounds good to me." Derek eyed Fredrick who lifted the corner of his mouth.

"Okay. Good work, Fredrick. Derek, keep us posted."

"Will do."

The meeting broke up, and Derek followed Fredrick to his office to find a mutual time they could meet. He was excited about what the R&D team was working on. These new technologies could be good not only for Vigers, but for their customers too.

~

Lexi lay in bed lounging for a few minutes before her alarm went off. Her phone dinged with a text from Derek: **Did you hear? Stiletto filed bankruptcy.**

Her eyes widened. Had she read that right? *Wow!*

Well, you reap what you sow, she thought. She smirked.

She ran through the week in her head—thought about her meetings, and of course she thought about Derek. She had to admit, spending time with him was good. It felt different than all the other guys she'd dated. He wasn't pushy and yet somehow found a way to stretch her boundaries. She'd really need to keep an eye on that, but as far as her number one priority—sex—she hoped it would never end.

She stared at the ceiling. Then, it occurred to Lexi that she hadn't had her period in a while. *Probably any day now.*

She didn't pay much attention to the color of her pills. She took one every day; it was that simple.

Out of curiosity, she yanked her purse off the floor and pulled out her pill pack.

Oh, crap! She was late—three days late. Well, shit. She was never late, especially since taking the pill. Her heartrate sped. She threw back the covers and got ready for work. She had a stop to make along the way.

Lexi cruised the aisle in the drugstore and picked the first pregnancy kit she could get her hands on, then checked out. She scanned the directions on the box as she sat in her car. It read to complete the test first thing in the morning.

Be calm, she told herself. It could be a false alarm.

What the hell would she do if she were pregnant?

At the office, her cell phone dinged as she turned on her PC. It was from Derek, wishing her a good morning.

She replied because she wanted to do a pre-emptive strike in case he got suspicious about anything. She really didn't want to talk to him until she knew something for certain.

Hi. Busy day today and tomorrow. I'll call you later. Have a good day.

That should work.

She had twenty minutes before her first meeting. She dialed Rachel's office line.

"Hi," Rachel answered in her very cheery voice.

"Am I on speaker?"

"No."

"I'm late."

"Late? As in late late? You're never late."

"I know and I'm freaking out."

"Don't. It could just be stress, hormones, a million things."

"Like pregnancy."

"Okay, a million *other* things. Did you buy a test?"

"Yes. I have to take it first thing in the morning." She strummed her fingers on her desk.

Shit! Did this mean she'd had to give up wearing heels?

"Don't freak out. Do you want me to come over tonight? Hunter can watch the kids."

Lexi hated being needy, but she also knew she'd be climbing the walls. "Yeah, that would be good."

"Okay, text me when you're leaving the office and I'll meet you at your place."

She disconnected the line and tried to take a deep breath. Several times. Her body relaxed a smidge. She'd have to focus on work as much as she could so she didn't think about what might be growing in her body.

Rachel arrived just after six. Lexi couldn't concentrate anymore, so whatever she had lingering needed to wait until the next day, like scrutinizing more portfolios so Tonia could set up interviews.

"Hey. How're you doing?" Rachel wrapped her arms around her.

"Eh."

"Why don't we cook dinner?"

"I'm not really hungry." Lexi shrugged her shoulders. Her nerves killed her appetite.

"I understand, but it will distract you." Rachel laid her bag on the sofa and went to the kitchen to scrounge around in the fridge. In a matter of minutes, she had the ingredients out for chicken cacciatore. "Here, cut this pepper."

Rachel went about doing her part, occasionally giving another task to Lexi. Rachel was right; it did distract her. And the kitchen smelled incredible. In no time, they were seated at her dining table eating the meal.

"So," Rachel broke the silence, "have you thought about what you'll do if it's positive?"

Lexi really wanted a glass of red wine, but bless her sweet friend, Rachel didn't even offer. She just poured two glasses of water like it was nothing new.

"No. I'm almost forty and never thought kids were in my future. Hell, I don't think I ever wanted kids."

Rachel tilted her head to the side. "And now?"

"Well, I still don't think I do. I mean, maybe it has

everything to do with the lousy example I had for parents. I also never had that mothering instinct."

Her friend nodded. Kids were perfect for Rachel; she was a great mom. Lexi was content just being an aunt.

"Do you plan to talk to Derek?"

She absolutely needed to talk to Derek. He'd played a part in this, after all. But... "I think I'll wait until after I know for sure."

"I bet he'd be an awesome father," Rachel said in a low tone.

Lexi couldn't know for sure. But talking to him was critical, but she'd need to work up to it if the test came back positive. There were so many questions. How would he react? Would he be mad or happy? Maybe he'd call it off...the relationship or whatever they had. Nowhere in the rules was there a contingency for pregnancy.

Oh, she could imagine that: *In cases of pregnancy, we drop our lives, throw out the rules, and head straight to a preacher.*

She sighed into her water glass. Tomorrow. She'd have more answers tomorrow.

The women finished dinner and found a movie to watch on TV. Any time the thought about being pregnant popped in her head, she forced it out. There was nothing she could do until she took the damn test. And the lack of control over the situation was making her damn-near insane.

At ten o'clock, Rachel hugged her goodbye and wished

her luck. "Call me in the morning."

As the sun rose in some far-off place, Lexi wished she was in that far-off place too. She'd had a fitful sleep. She gathered her wits for a minute and then climbed out of bed. She walked into the bathroom where the test was open and on the counter, ready for use. She studied the directions one last time, squatted over the toilet, and sent up a silent prayer.

She waited the allotted minutes without even attempting to look, but when the timer on her phone chimed, she lifted the stick.

Oh God!

She slowly sank to the bathroom floor.

No, this can't be happening.

Positive.

Her breath turned shallow. How did this happen? She took her pills religiously. What could she do? What were her options?

Oh Lord. Pregnant at forty.

A tear streamed down her cheek unbidden.

She shook her head and turned on the shower. She needed to get ready for work. She had a company to run. Forty-five minutes later, she was out the door and calling Rachel from the car.

Rachel answered on the first ring. "I've been on pins and needles. What did it say?"

"It's positive." Lexi felt the tears well in her eyes again.

"Oh wow," Rachel breathed out. "How are you? What can I do?"

"Well, in shock." She let out a shaky breath. "And nothing right now, but thanks, babe. I need a little time and space. I gotta figure this thing out."

"Okay, but I'm calling you later to check up on you."

She smiled. Her friend was a mother through and through. "All right."

Lexi ended the call, and by the time she made it to her office, she had her obstetrician's office on the line.

Damn! Her doctor's first availability was a week away. Lexi scheduled the appointment and stared out the window at nothing.

Absently, she laid a hand over her belly. She'd never imagined she'd been in this position. She never had the "mothering gene" and that was fine with her. Dillion and any other boyfriends she'd been serious with hadn't challenged her choice or pushed her to change her mind. Well, now it was like her mind was getting changed without her.

She dropped her head in her hands and let the weight collapse to the desk. There was one person she needed to talk to. Derek.

God knew how he was going to react. *Fuck!*

She buzzed Tonia.

"Lexi."

"Tonia, I'm not feeling well. Would you please reschedule my appointments? I'm going home."

"Sure, no problem. I hope you feel better."

She sat in her car at the office building's parking garage, pulled out Derek's business card, and typed the address for Vigers headquarters into her GPS.

After a forty-minute drive, she arrived. Lexi took a fortifying breath. She had no earthly idea what she was going to say, but she had to tell him. If nothing else, he had to know.

Stepping off the elevator on the sixth floor, she observed her surroundings. This would be what many called "mahogany row." Here was where the execs, the hootie whos, worked.

A receptionist in a designer suit with perfect hair and makeup met Lexi's gaze. "May I help you?"

She pushed back her shoulders and softened her facial muscles. "Yes. I'm looking for Derek Hollister."

"Splendid. He's down that hall, the last door on the left."

"Thank you." Lexi arrived at his section of the floor. Plush carpet, expensive furniture, and enough space to throw a party for the entire Salvation Army. *Gees! This is a profitable company, to say the least.*

Lexi approached his assistant's desk.

"May I help you?" a gray-haired woman with a no-nonsense stare asked.

"Yes, I'm here to see Derek Hollister. I'm Alexis King. I don't have an appointment, but I think he'll want to see me."

The woman's expression gave nothing away as she pushed back from her desk. "One moment, please."

The assistant walked the short distance to his office. Lexi heard talking but couldn't make out the words. In a fraction of a second, the assistant and Derek strode out of the office.

"Lexi." He leaned down and kissed her cheek. "I'm so glad to see you. This is unexpected. Please come in."

He looked so beautiful she wanted to cry.

Cry? Oh, God. Lexi never cried. Could it be from all the hormones? She followed him into his office.

He closed the door behind her and furrowed his brow. "Is something wrong?"

"Derek, can we sit?"

"Sure." He motioned to the davenport along the wall, and she sank down against the supple leather. She wondered how many catnaps he'd had on this sofa. He sat facing her and waited.

She inhaled. "Derek, I got some news, news that I wasn't expecting, that I need to share with you."

He held her hand. She was so out of her depth that she let him. "I'm a few days late with my period, so I took a test. I'm pregnant."

He squeezed her hand, and his eyes twinkled. He didn't pull away. "I take it you're upset about this."

"Of course, I'm upset." Tears streamed down her cheeks. She'd managed to keep it together for over a day, and now in front of him, she was crying. She tugged free, rose, and paced the carpet. "I'm too old to bear a child."

And what of him? In his mid-forties, he would hardly want to start a family, right?

Maybe there was a tiny part of Lexi that hoped he might, but she squashed it. This was no time for fairytales. This was time for practical, straight-forward thinking.

Derek didn't know what to say to Lexi. Secretly, he was thrilled. He was forty-five himself, and never thought he'd be a father. Never had aspired to it. But if Lexi was the mother of his child or children, he was all in. One hundred percent.

She paced the room, and he bit his tongue. He wanted to say, *That's great. We're having a baby!*

On the other hand, she seemed to be having an entire conversation with herself, her back to him as she went on and on about not planning on being a mom.

"Lexi, please sit down," he pleaded after her fifth go around the office. "We can figure this out."

She stopped pacing and met his gaze head-on. "Derek, I'm leaving now. I need some time. Please don't call me."

He stood and she stepped back. Tears continued down her cheeks. "Lexi, please. We can talk, if not now, tonight. I'll come over."

She shook her head. "I need time. I'll call you."

She clutched her bag to her chest and spun around. She was gone in a flash.

He sank back down on the sofa, exhaled, and rested his head in his hands. *God, please, bring her back to me. Please don't let this be the end.*

He could be a father. If he was a father, he would embrace the role wholeheartedly. He was in. But all he really wanted was Lexi. *This can't tear us apart. It can't!*

Chapter Fifteen

DEREK GREETED FREDRICK as he walked into his office Wednesday morning and sat in the chair across from him at the round conference table. They were tasked to review the numbers for amping up data security hardware, something Derek felt strongly about, as strongly as Fredrick. Yet Lexi was front and center in his mind.

She'd stormed into his office the day before and dropped a bomb on him. It was a bomb, in a way, but it wasn't the end of the world. He could already imagine how amazing it would be. He'd happily sell the condo and move all of them into a house with a white picket fence.

He'd have a chance to raise a family the proper way. He'd teach his son how to be a man and a husband. Or he'd teach his daughter what to look for in a future husband. How to tell the bad ones from the good ones.

He wanted it all—if Lexi wanted it. He knew she was grappling with that decision. He would support her in whatever she chose; he just couldn't lose her over this. She was the main priority for him.

But right then, he had to find a way to make sure the numbers made sense for the executive staff to approve the expenditure and write it into the budget. Getting these monies approved and allocated would be the necessary step to take Vigers to the next level in the world of corporate infrastructure and networking. This would ensure their success.

Lexi took her time getting into the office that morning. She didn't have any early meetings, so she pondered her future in a low-key vibe. Very unlike her. Somehow everything seemed different. The sun had been bright that morning, which anyone would expect in the summertime, but the fresh scent in the air downright confused Lexi. Usually, Houston in August was oppressive—hot as hades and humid.

She hadn't slept as badly as she'd worried she might. Of course, all she thought about now was the life growing inside her, and Derek. She recalled the hurt in his eyes the prior day when she'd asked for space to sort this out. As much as he'd tried to school his expression, the hurt was there. Additionally, to Lexi's huge surprise, he wasn't upset.

She would have placed money down that he'd jump back, possibly even yell. She'd have bet *he'd* be the one to distance himself. Well, regardless of hurt feelings, she needed time to come to terms with this. Lexi didn't want to force

Derek into a marriage he'd never intended. Hell, she didn't know if *she* wanted to get married, let alone be a mom.

She had six more days before her doctor's appointment when she'd get more information, and she couldn't wait. She wanted to talk to a professional and learn all she could about how women in their forties carried a baby. Reading the internet was an option, but she didn't think she could handle any horror stories right now.

There were ways to fix this. Lexi frankly wasn't taking anything off the table at this point, but what if? She found herself asking that question over and over.

What if she wanted to be a mother after all? What if she could be a good mother? What if she had a boy like Derek? What if Derek wanted a baby? What if he wanted to get married and make a family with her?

In less than a day, her head swam for completely different reasons than her business.

As Lexi strode to the building's cafeteria for lunch, her phone rang. *Rachel.*

Her bestie had been a godsend, calling her regularly and checking up on her.

"How ya' doin' today?" Rachel asked.

"Actually, not too bad." Lexi took a seat in the corner of the lobby. People passed by, coming and going, and no one paid any attention to her. She could have a conversation and not worry about being overheard.

"Glad to hear it. Have you heard from Derek?"

"No, I suspect he'll give me some time and space like I asked." She trusted that he'd keep his word. "I'm just..."

After a bit, Rachel asked, "Just what?"

"I don't know. Rachel, what if I wanted to have it? What if I could carry this baby to term?"

"It is possible. Women do it all the time. Plus, you're healthy, and there's probably no reason you couldn't have a perfectly healthy baby. They have blood tests to monitor certain age-related issues." Rachel's voice turned softer as she said, "I guess I didn't think you'd even be interested."

"I know. Me either. But I kinda think the idea is growing on me. I saw a woman jogging on the sidewalk this morning, pushing a baby stroller. And I thought to myself, that could be me. I could totally do that."

Rachel chuckled. "Lexi, you can do anything you set your mind to, that's the thing about you. Do you think Derek would be open to that?"

"I actually think he would. He didn't throw me out when I told him yesterday."

"Right."

"Rach, I'm just sayin' that I'm not gonna make any rash decisions at this point. I'll meet with my doctor and take it from there."

"Good plan. Wanna come over for dinner tonight?"

She sighed. That sounded absolutely perfect. "Yes, that would be great. Let me bring some dessert, even if only the rug rats eat it."

Rachel laughed. "Okay, babe. See you later."

Lexi stashed her phone into her purse and went to order her usual salad with grilled chicken. Fifteen minutes later, she carried her lunch and unsweetened tea back to her office but froze at the door.

A huge bouquet of flowers sat on her desk.

She spun around and met Tonia's gaze. Her assistant said, "They arrived ten minutes ago."

Lexi nodded and made her way to the arrangement, their fragrance already filling the air in her office. She knew they were from Derek, and she lifted the card to read. Wow! Except it was more than a card, it was a letter.

Alexis,

I know this isn't what you planned but know that I support and stand by your decision with our child. You will not be alone in this.

I have a sense that life has thrown you a few curve balls along the way. I told you I didn't want to "fix" you and I meant it. We're all broken in some form or fashion. You are who you are because of the life you led. One day, maybe you'll trust me enough to tell me all about it.

Until then, I'm here, patiently waiting, whenever you want to talk.

I won't use the L-word for the first time in a letter,

Derek

She chuckled through the tears streaming down her cheeks. That was such an incredible letter. He loved her. He'd said he would stand beside her. What more could a woman ask for?

Normally, the thought of marriage post-Dillion would cause Lexi to break out in a cold sweat. Derek didn't specifically say he would marry her, but she knew in her gut. She knew he'd want to raise this baby together, live together, and grow old together.

And for the first time in a long time, she felt it too—she wanted it too.

She neatly refolded the letter, slipped it back into its envelope, and slid it into her purse.

She would text him a thank you later since she'd blown most of her lunchtime and only had ten minutes to eat before her next appointment. Gregory was going on a nice, long paid vacation. Whether he wanted to or not.

She chuckled out loud and the laughter dried her tears.

After her quick lunch, Lexi met with Gregory and gently filled him in on the errors she'd found.

Shock showed on his face. "Am I fired? Are you mad?"

"Gregory, you are not fired and I'm not mad." She reconsidered. "Well, I am."

His eyebrows rose to his hairline and his face paled.

"I'm mad at myself for letting you work while your vacation time accumulated. I should have just thrown you on a plane to Barbados with nothing but a credit card and sunscreen."

He chuckled as his eyes grew misty.

She continued, "I know where your loyalty lies. I know for a fact you want nothing but the best for AK. But you're no good to me burned out. Get it?"

He lowered his head and nodded.

"So, the last fiscal year crap is done, and the budget is approved for this year, so please go on vacation. Go to the mountains or the beach or both—I don't care. You've earned it."

"Yes, ma'am," he said in a soft joking tone.

Great. Lexi hugged the man and sent him on his way. And now her damn eyes were floating. Iced tea always did that to her.

She strode to the ladies' room, went about her business, and gasped when she looked at her underwear. She prayed no one heard.

She'd gotten her period. It was her true period. She'd read about spotting that could happen during pregnancy; this wasn't that.

What she'd thought had been possible morning queasiness that morning, had actually been her period. What did she know? She'd never been pregnant before.

And that was the crux of it. She wasn't pregnant. Probably never had been. It was a false positive on the test. Also, a possibility.

Lexi sat on the commode for several more minutes,

trying to gather her chaotic thoughts before she walked backed to her office. She wasn't pregnant.

She should be relieved, but instead a sadness crept over her. Had she actually been looking forward to this? Wasn't it just two days ago that she'd been freaking out about the possibility of having a baby? And now, she didn't have to worry about it. She should be happy.

A tear landed on the back of her hand. She hadn't realized she could cry over this.

She pulled herself together and made her way back to her office.

Phoning Tonia to let her know she'd be out the rest of the day, Lexi got her things together to head home. Work was no place to be while on an emotional rollercoaster.

Once she was home and in her sanctuary, she texted Rachel: **I got my period.** ☹

Rachel replied: **I can be there in 30 minutes.**

Lexi hadn't cried so much in years, not since she caught Dillion cheating on her a few months before they were to be married.

Rachel sat next to her on the sofa and set down the tissue box beside her. "Have you spoken to Derek?"

She shrugged her shoulder. She wanted to talk to him but didn't know what to say. "First, I'm upset because I think I'm pregnant. Now I'm upset because I'm not pregnant. He's gonna think I'm crazy."

Rachel pressed her lips together and tipped her head. "He won't. He just needs to know, that's all." After a brief pause, she said, "You love him, don't you?"

Lexi met her friend's gaze. "I...um...I think I do. I've wanted to deny it, but that doesn't make it any less true. I didn't want to fall in love. Being in love means pain, at least for me—don't argue, it's true."

Rachel gripped her hand. "I knew it. I knew you loved him. You've been happier than you've been in a long time. Love does not equal pain. Try not to lump him in with the past assholes in your life—Dillion, Bryan, or your controlling stepfather. None of them understood about real love or relationships. Derek does and he thinks the world of you." She squeezed Lexi's fingers.

"Yeah, I was happy and now I'm miserable again." Lexi blotted the tears beneath her eyes. "If he's smart, he'll run for the hills."

"Hush." Rachel pulled her in close for a comforting hug.

Lexi needed to talk to Derek, and she prayed she hadn't scared him away.

"I need to use the restroom and then I'll get us some wine." Rachel went back to the bathroom.

Life is full of curveballs, Lex. You've had worse. Adjust so you can move on.

After a few minutes, Rachel returned with two glasses of white wine. "You sit and take it easy. I'll make some dinner for us."

She heard Rach banging around in the kitchen and thought she'd better get up and help her friend rather than wallow any longer. "What'cha making?"

"Just a casserole. It'll take an hour in the oven but it's still early, so we have time."

"What can I do?"

"Chop this onion." Rachel placed an onion with a cutting board in front of her.

Lexi didn't know how Rachel managed to make a feast. A little of this, a little of that, and before long, a covered casserole was in the oven. Anytime Lexi cooked anything with more than 3 ingredients, she needed a recipe book.

The doorbell rang.

Lexi sighed. Hopefully it was just a delivery. She was in no mood to talk to anyone now.

"Let me get it," Rachel offered and made the short walk to the door.

In a split second, she called to Lexi, "Uh, babe, I think these are for you."

Lexi jumped off the barstool and turned toward the door. Someone stood at the entry, holding another huge bouquet of flowers.

He lowered the vase to reveal his face, and those mesmerizing hazel eyes.

Derek.

Chapter Sixteen

DEREK STARED DOWN at Lexi, his heart warming at the red in her eyes—a giveaway that she'd been crying.

When Rachel had called his office and told him Lexi wasn't pregnant and was distraught, he'd dropped everything to come over. He'd stopped at his favorite florist—who'd been getting a lot of business from him lately—to buy some flowers to help cheer her up.

"Hi," he said to Lexi, then faced Rachel. "Thanks."

"You're welcome. Dinner is in the oven, when the timer goes off, take it out." Rachel wrapped an arm around Lexi. "You're in good hands. I'll call you tomorrow." Rachel picked up her bag and nodded at him before leaving, closing the door behind her.

Lexi still hadn't said a word.

He placed the flowers on her table and approached her, clasping her hands in his, and leaned down to kiss her forehead. "I'm sorry," he murmured.

Her lower lip quivered. "I thought I'd be relieved. It was

just a false alarm."

He brought her hands to his mouth to kiss her knuckles. "Yeah, sounds like it. Rachel called me so I came right over."

"I gathered that." She glanced up at him through her damp lashes. "How about we sit?"

"Okay." They sat on her sofa. He kept a hold of her hands; he desperately wanted to maintain their connection, even if she didn't return the pressure.

Her chest rose and fell with her inhale and exhale. "I've had quite a few dickheads in my life who sorta jacked with my heart."

He wasn't sure where this was going, but maybe she was ready to trust him with the truth of why she was so guarded, especially when it came to men.

"It started with my stepfather who was nasty and verbally abusive. An adult bully. My mother wasn't strong enough to stand up to him. Some days I felt like a complete loser, like I could do nothing right. As soon as I could get out of that house I did. Rachel was my rock. Still is."

Derek could relate to her story of her mother. Sometimes, he wondered if wives really understood the power they had over their husbands. The power to persuade them to the right thing.

"Then, I dated Bryan who cheated on me. I healed and put myself back out there, and that's when I met Dillion. We dated for a year, and he proposed. Two months before our wedding I caught him cheating."

"Asshole."

"I thought we were in love. I thought he loved and cared about me." She exhaled. "I guess there's only so much heartbreak a person can take. Or at least so much *I* can take."

Derek kissed her hands again. "Babe, I want your heartache to be over. Know that I'm not like those men."

She glanced down at her hands. "From that point on, I kept my relationships purely physical. There were no expectations of a future together. And frankly it was working for me. Until I met you."

He listened calmly, hoping he'd like where this was going.

"This whole pregnancy thing threw me for a loop and made me question just about everything."

Derek nodded. He could believe that. She'd probably wondered about raising a child while running a company. She'd probably worried about how he'd felt and would he want to marry her? Of course, that's assuming she would even warm up to the idea herself.

After the pause stretched, he asked, "Want to know what I think? I think you did the best you could with what you'd been dealt by the assholes in your life. In fact, based on the success of your company, you did more than just survive, you thrived."

She looked up to meet his gaze.

"If you don't know how I feel, I love you. I love your sass, your tenacity, your desire to do what's right. I think we deserve a shot at a relationship."

She bit her lips together and scrunched her forehead.

"I know you're scared, Lex. How else are we going to know if we have a future unless we try?"

"I'm not perfect," she countered.

"Neither am I."

"I have baggage."

"Don't we all?" He knelt down before her. It made it easier to meet her gaze since she'd been looking down already. He stroked her thighs and pecked her lips. "I want you. I want *only* you. I don't want to fuck you for a night. I want to fuck you for life."

Her eyes were trained on his. He didn't blink. He could see that she debated his words, weighing if he was worth the risk.

"Okay."

"Okay?"

She gave a small smile. "Yeah. We can give it a try."

He leaned in and kissed her warm lips.

She felt like heaven. She kissed him back and opened for him.

He clasped her beautiful face as he maneuvered between her legs to get closer. He slowly pushed into the back of the sofa, and her arms wrapped around him.

One delicate hand stroked the side of his face, and she broke the kiss. "I love you too, Derek. I didn't want to, but you made me fall in love with you." She smiled, and nothing could be more perfect.

This was all he wanted. He'd spend the rest of his life showing her she was special and worthy of love.

He reclined her slightly to lean against the back of the sofa. As he shifted his body over hers, she wrapped a leg around his. He stroked her bare thigh and resuming kissing her, guiding his tongue along hers.

The little vixen managed to wiggle her fingers in between them and start unbuttoning his shirt. She pulled it out of his waistband, finished the job, and pushed it off his shoulders.

He rose to take it the rest of the way and toed off his shoes. Reaching for her buttons, he gave her the same routine.

As she threw her blouse to the floor, he slipped beneath her and unfastened her skirt, pushing it down her legs.

God, she was beautiful. His cock strained against his pants, anxious for release but more anxious for her. He needed to be inside her, or he'd die.

He kissed her neck and slipped her bra straps off her shoulders, crushing his lips to her peaked nipples.

She moaned over his head and arched her back, demanding more. Her fingers wove through his hair as he loved on her full breasts.

His hand drifted southward, dancing over the lace of her panties before slipping under and weaving through her wet slit.

Fuck! He loved how wet she got for him.

He lifted his head. "Alexis," he whispered, "were you sad when you learned that you weren't pregnant?"

Her breath hitched as her eyes flew open. "Yes, but I don't want to talk about that now."

He smiled inside and continued his gentle torture. "I thought so."

She writhed beneath him, and he only gave it a brief minute when he stopped.

He stood and did a quick search to find her purse sitting on the counter.

"What are you doing?" her voice rose at the end of the question.

He reached into her purse, found her pack of pills, walked to the kitchen, and tossed them in the garbage can.

"Hey."

"You won't need those anymore."

She tried narrowing her eyes at him to hide the twinkle, but she couldn't fool him.

Derek stalked back her way, loosening the hold of his pants. He swooped down, lifting her in his arms. Then stepping her back to the wall, in one easy movement, he ripped her panties off her, pinned her up against the wall and drove home.

"Ah," she called out as he pierced through her incredible wet heat. "Derek, my period."

"I don't care." He plunged, building their climb

together.

"You're mine, Lexi. Say it."

She panted with every thrust he took. She wouldn't be long. "Yes, Derek. I'm yours."

"I love you. And we'll be together for the rest of our lives, but know the rule still applies."

"What rule?" Her chest heaved as she climbed closer to ecstasy.

"Anytime. Anywhere." He reached down for her swollen clit and massaged it lightly, tipping her over the edge.

She called out his name and writhed in his arms as her climax crashed through her.

He did the same, letting his seed fill her. If she wanted a baby, he would give her one.

He hauled her close but didn't pull out. He stepped out of his pants and carried her to the bedroom. Her legs clasped around his waist. He laid them down on her bed, never breaking their connection. Slowly, he resumed his thrusts inside her. He may never be soft again as long as Lexi was in his life.

"What are you doing?" she whispered.

"Making love to you. I fucked you out there, but now we take it slow. I want you to never doubt that you mean the world to me. These last few months have been incredible, and I want it to continue. Can you handle that?"

"Yes." The smile on her face grew.

He pulled out and kissed his way down her soft body,

eager to give her another orgasm. His tongue claimed her delicate bundle of nerves and a finger gently stroked her lips, gathering the combined fluids from their lovemaking, spreading it around. "Lift your knees up, Alexis."

She bent her knees and rested her feet on the mattress. She opened for him wider in this position, and he couldn't wait to bring her more pleasure.

With the moisture on his finger, he slid his finger south, dragging the moisture to her tiny hole.

She moaned.

He knew she'd like a little ass play—if she would trust him. He continued licking and circling over her clit as his finger made another swipe through her slit to wet his finger more. Sliding one last time over her tight hole, he gently pushed his wet finger through the tight barrier.

"Derek, no." She pushed on his shoulders meekly, even as her back bowed at the new sensation.

He lifted his head an inch. "Trust me, baby. You'll like this, and I have just five minutes left before that oven timer goes off." He continued his gentle push-pull inside her. "Five minutes to bring you to orgasm. Five minutes to make you feel good." His mouth claimed her pussy again.

"Yes, Derek. Make me feel good."

Absolutely, precious. For the rest of my life.

Sneak Peak

Coming in Fall of 2021, The Kaleidoscope Series

Excerpt from Angel In White

THEY ARRIVED SAFELY back at his place. Before Aidan got out of the car, Maurice leaned over and gasped his shirt, pulling Aidan close. He pressed his lips to Aidan's who opened for him. He cupped his jaw, diving into Aidan's warm mouth, tasting the masculine flavor was intoxicating. The lust, the fire, that pulsed through his veins only Aidan could put out. Aidan was a balm on his heart and soul. Their passions were equally matched, and for that, Maurice felt blessed.

He broke the kiss long enough to say, "Let's go inside."

Maurice stumbled in a misstep up the curb and laughed. Aidan smiled and took his hand. "You got this, baby?"

He grinned.

Inside, Maurice slipped off his shoes. "I need to use the bathroom. I'll be right back."

As he came out, Aidan came down the hall. "Be right out. I'll meet you on the sofa," he whispered so as not to awaken Vicki.

Maurice walked, following his hand along the wall to keep his balance. When he came to Vicki's door, the last door before the great room, when he noticed it was cracked open slightly. He couldn't resist. He pushed it open to peer inside.

Just as he'd suspected. She slept sprawled out in the center of her queen-size bed. The moonlight creeping in from the window made her look like an angel. He stepped closer, watching in awe as she slept on her stomach, draped in a white sheet, her brown hair cascading over her pillow.

"What are you doing in here?" Aidan whispered from over his shoulder.

"Look at her. She looks like an angel," he whispered back.

"C'mon. Let's not wake her."

Maurice heard the words, but didn't let it register. Instead he stepped closer, now inches from her bed.

Aidan looped a finger in his jeans waistband and tugged, wordlessly trying to get him to obey, but Maurice was rooted.

He watched the gentle rise and fall of her back as she breathed. *Beautiful.*

He reached for the white sheet, carefully peeling it back.

Aidan tugged harder, but it didn't matter. He already saw her angelic body—face down, arms under her pillow, wearing nothing but a white lace thong.

Maurice looked up at Aidan whose mouth gapped at the vision before them. "She's beautiful."

Other Books by Mia London

Honeymoon Hideaway

Runaway (Cascade Mountain Manhunt, 1)
Renegade (Cascade Mountain Manhunt, 2)

Accidental Tryst

Life To The Max
Wanton Angel, Prequel to Life To The Max

Perfect Seduction (Perfect, 1)
Perfect Surrender (Perfect, 2)

Beyond Lace (Hard Men of the Rockies, 4)

About the Author

Mia London loves to write.

After reading fiction for years, she decided it was finally time to put those images and scenes floating around in her head down on paper.

She is a huge fan of romance, highly optimistic, and wildly faithful to the HEA (happily ever after). Her goal is to create a fantasy you will enjoy with characters you could love.

She lives in Texas with her attentive, loving, super-model husband, and perfectly behaved, brilliant children. Her produce never wilts, there are no weeds in her flowerbeds and chocolate is her favorite food group.

Facebook

Twitter

Instagram

Goodreads

www.mialondon.com

Email: mia@mialondon.com